NO ONE

KNOWS THEIR

BLOOD TYPE

No One Knows Their Blood Type
FIRST EDITION
Text copyright © Maya Abu Al-Hayyat, 2013
English translation copyright © Hazem Jamjoum, 2024

Originally published in Arabic as
La Ahad Ya'rif Zumrat Damih by Dar al-Adab, Beirut (2013)

Printed in the United States of America
ISBN 979·8·9897084·1·3

DESIGN ≈ SEVY PEREZ
Text in Brandon Grotesque & Adobe Caslon Pro

COVER & INTERIOR COVER ART
The Gathering by Malak Mattar (2019, acrylic on canvas)

This book is published by the
Cleveland State University Poetry Center
csupoetrycenter.com
2121 Euclid Avenue, Cleveland, Ohio 44115-2214

A CATALOG RECORD FOR THIS TITLE IS
AVAILABLE FROM THE LIBRARY OF CONGRESS

NO ONE KNOWS THEIR BLOOD TYPE

MAYA ABU AL-HAYYAT

translated by Hazem Jamjoum

Jumana

Jerusalem, 2007

Malika, the midwife of East Jerusalem, dies. I scrub her with cheap wine. I scrub every part of her, but I can't close her half-shut eyes or stop her glance wandering off to something else. She still wants to see everything, to make sure everyone is where they're meant to be, doing what they ought to be doing. We try to do what she would have done in our place. We try and we fail. No one can be on top of everything like she always was. If she knew she'd be in a freezer until Monday she'd have thrown a fit and done everything in her power to prevent it. No one is thinking about that now; everyone is busy with the preparations. We try not to think about how it is Malika herself that we're clothing with the white socks and satin chemise she would have bought especially for a day like today.

Her body, shriveled and dehydrated, is heavy now. The three of us try to lift her but we can't. I try not to look at her private parts, but the few little hairlets sprouting there catch my eye. Her face yellowed on the left side from exsanguination, red blotches on her forearm, two pale breasts floundering right and left: everything dead, for a while now, and resisting.

She does not want to die, she doesn't.

This woman from the Greek community who birthed half the men and women of Jerusalem and never gave birth to anyone herself, she lies before me in a barren room, a room on the floor of death in Hadassah Hospital. I, who stumbled on her by chance, never imagined that it would be me among those preparing her for departure, let alone be the one to choose her last dress, a dress she might not even like.

I exit the room, leaving Nina and Um 'Aziz with that body, its metamorphosis into a white ghost complete. Nina has primped her sister's cold lips with some of her fuchsia lipstick, like they did in the eighties, making Malika look like a Geisha doll. Suheil is outside trying to call someone to arrange the prayer service and the burial. I try to console him, but he doesn't seem the type that needs it. From the moment the Hebrew-accented Arabic of the Mizrahi nurse announced Malika's death, Suheil had diagnosed its cause as water in the lungs, failure of the heart, clogging of the arteries. He'd come to terms with the matter without any need of my sympathies.

I've only known Malika for the past two weeks. My father had been admitted to the Maqased Hospital for open-heart surgery, which sent him into a state of clinical death, so he had to be moved here to Hadassah. His state has not changed since. It was not only the hospital that brought me and Malika together, but also a glance I shared with Suheil, who had joined his mother and aunt in the move from their home to the hospital room. Both Malika and Nina had left no uncertainty as to the fact that Suheil had spent the past five years in search of a wife. The search that has now accompanied him into his sixth decade.

I didn't need more than that glance to know I would share a lifetime with this man. That was all I could think whenever I saw him, whether he was drinking that American coffee I can't stand, or in the hospital hallway, or seated at Malika's bedside and getting ready to leave.

I started to visit her as an escape from my regimen of waiting for my father to either wake up or die, hoping to see Suheil, who visited at the same hour every evening. My own visits became a near daily activity: I'd sit beside Nina, who would follow Malika's instructions like a robot. I would sit there trying to fathom this woman on her deathbed, with a heart that burned with the fire of a twenty-year-old, and whose ambitions in life remained... everything.

Everyone in the geriatric ward loved Malika. Everyone introduced her to their visitors, children and grandchildren, including the woman who wore a thick woolly cap on her head and only spoke in Hebrew.

Malika listened to their stories so she could tell her own, thoroughly describing the aches and pains that stretched from her nose, ulcerated by two oxygen tubes, to her legs, swollen with edema. She never forgot to add a deep and breathy "*aakh*" after each sentence, a sound emanating from the merciless itch of her psoriasis or the pain of the eroded cartilage that had bowed her spine, shrinking her to the size of a small boy.

Everyone in the room knew Malika's medical chart by heart and could recite her life story, beginning with her work as a registered midwife at the Hospice Hospital in the early '50s, all the way to her weekly visits to Hadassah over the past three years to rest her waterlogged legs. Both male and female nurses treated her like an authority who would determine whether they'd passed or failed a performance review. She gave them unflinching advice on the world of nursing in her not-bad-at-all English, never failing to wink at the young handsome nurse who bathed her every other day, assuring him with the occasional "I'm like your mother." He responded each time with a big hearty laugh and a small cheeky kiss.

The smell of cleaning liquids, medicine, and the geriatric feces that saturated the cloths and bedpans didn't discourage any of us from our evening visits. Nor did the smell prevent me from escaping my father's lifeless room to

9

this other one with its soulful verve. No one visits him and the evening hours at his bedside are disconsolate. This other room is inhabited by four women, and though one neither wakes up nor receives visitors, the groans of the rest are regularly silenced by the new stories carried in with visitors who tell them.

People don't visit my father because anyone who would consider dropping by is not allowed to enter Jerusalem. No one visits the other man who shares his room, either. This other man doesn't speak with us, as if frightened by our very presence. If you discount the incessant phone calls, the only words spoken in that room are those of me and Yara pestering each other, and the slumbered mutterings of the other man calling for someone in the Hebrew neither of us understands. Together these sounds are the background music to the thoughts in our heads. Yara leaves every evening to return to her children and husband, the man behind the incessant phone calls (calls motivated by jealousy not love). I am left with them: two alien men, one of them my father.

Malika passed away this evening. Visitation hours hadn't yet started. Nina wasn't there, and neither was Suheil, nor I, not even the handsome nurse. They tried to resuscitate her for a long time, hoping someone would come who could make things easier for that soul of hers that refused to leave. Nina had gone with Suheil for a change of clothes, but by the time they got back to the hospital it was all over. They saw her through the window that looks out into the hallway. I was there too, as if we had all agreed to arrive at the same moment. We all saw the glance in our direction. The look was not one of reproach, or joy, or even sadness. It was a glance that wandered in silence, death for a woman who was never silent.

Yara calls my cell phone to tell me off for interfering in the life of her family, and for leaving her alone with our father. She wants to go shopping on Yafa

Street before heading home; she'd even said so that morning. I hurry to get to her before her anger drags us into another long unbearable conversation.

My father is still as he was: a large mass of surplus flesh with two oxygen tubes holding back his snores. Yara puts on what's left of her brand-name lipstick with the help of the mirror above the hospital-room sink. The other man watches as she, oblivious, picks up her imitation Gucci bag and rushes out of the room, warning me that she's in a hurry, and that I shouldn't call to nag her home. I sit on the plastic chair farthest from the two beds, grateful that she's finally left.

It's cold despite the infernal heat from the radiator they never shut off. Lately I've stopped looking at my father; his body is just another part of the room now, like the bed, the chair, and the window onto the maternity ward. On this day, though, my head tilts in his direction. I'm afraid he might suddenly wake up and ask about Yara, or scold me for my tight-fitting clothes.

His face is shrouded behind a dark shadow, and saliva drips from the corner of his lips. The wart on his temple has gotten bigger. I close my eyes so I don't have to see it, but another image appears from another time: my father sitting at the kitchen table in our home in El-Menzah V in Tunis with a smaller belly and less grey in his hair. He's preparing baguette sandwiches with hardboiled eggs that will trigger the exodus of all the students within a ten-meter radius the moment we open our lunch bags at school. He takes his time with the assembly, not forgetting the tomato slices and pickles that will make the eggs and the bread disgustingly soggy. A smile creeps onto my face, a smile that willfully ignores just how much I hated those sandwiches, how I considered them punishment.

I move between the sink and the edge of the bed, closing my eyes and thinking of a return to the world of Suheil and Malika. There is death there, but the life that is here is unbearable.

I open my eyes to familiar sounds, sounds I haven't heard in some time. Snores of a timbre I know well, but uncharacteristically long and uneven. All of a sudden, my father's body begins to convulse, as if it had swallowed a piece of metal it needed to disgorge. In that moment he does not seem like my father. He is a thing that resembles my father, and I am afraid to get near it. I gather my courage and approach him. I scream. I try to hold him down, to restrain him without touching the bullet wound in his chest from the Beirut days, but his body falls to the floor with a tremor that wakes up the entire ward and rips the oxygen tubes from his nostrils. For a moment he opens his eyes and releases a soulful snore.

For that quick moment, he seems almost comfortable. The nurses and everyone else rush in. They lift him using the bedsheet that tumbled to the floor with him. They try to resuscitate him with CPR and shocks from the defibrillator, but he has snorted his last snore.

That night my father's body is moved to the morgue to lie near Malika's, and Suheil and I join in the preparations. Unlike Suheil, though, I am an emotional wreck. The sight of my father—wrapped in a hospital sheet flapping in the hands of a nurse on either end of his corpse—was terrifying. More terrifying than anything else is trying and failing to reach Yara. She isn't answering her phone. Her permit only applies to the hospital's vicinity, and my mind spirals down the thought of soldiers arresting her. When I see them examining his body to fill in the death certificate with some remaining details, I fall. I collapse, exhausted by tears I can't explain.

I wake up in the emergency room of that same hospital. Suheil, looming with Yara above me, says I fell to the floor. They rushed me to the emergency room, where nurses carried out tests and found it was nothing more than a drop in my blood pressure. Yara is here, her face hovering over mine, her maquillage out of place pointing in every direction. And my father is someplace else.

There is so much we have to attend to now, and I still cannot believe that this man, this man who is my father, is gone from our lives forever. Is he really capable of dying? Do things this big actually die?

We sit on the ground floor of the hospital in silence. Yara calls my cousins in Amman and my father's friends in Ramallah so we can move him to Nablus for burial. In his worry for me, Suheil picked up my father's death certificate from the intensive care unit when he went to pick up his aunt's. He also picked up my test results.

Suheil sits reading through the reports to confirm that the causes he'd determined for my father's and his aunt's deaths were correct. He then speaks the sentence that will change everything. He utters these words without considering the fact that such sounds should not be uttered so casually, or with such naïveté. He says, as if pointing out a remarkable coincidence or a mere cosmic error:

"Your father's blood type is O positive, and yours is AB positive. That can't be right."

Jumana

Amman, 1986

I don't know which night I was conceived, but I do know that when nine months had passed, my life started to get complicated. All that I will relate here is not confirmed truth—these are stories I pass on from motley sources. None of them are entirely correct or straightforward; they follow the meandering intentions and motives of the storytellers.

My grandmother says my father threatened to raze their apartment building in the Mal'ab al-Baladi neighborhood of Beirut if they didn't give him their daughter as a bride. She hadn't yet turned seventeen, and was deeply in love with the neighbors' son, Omar. My aunt—my father's sister—says my maternal grandmother wanted some clout in the Sunni neighborhood that my father controlled; he was the military commander for el-Munazzameh there. And so she offered her daughter's hand to protect the drug dealer and thief that was her son, my uncle Ahmad. This same aunt also claims that when she would visit my mother's family in Beirut, she would stay in Uncle Ahmad's room and find suitcases filled with gold and jewelry under the bed.

What did happen, and this I don't doubt, was that they got married: him, an aspiring fida'i who'd left Palestine on donkey-back disguised under his mother's black cloak and head cover; her, a beauty from Beirut, the Paris of the East, who always wore the latest hairstyle, high heels and strapless dresses.

According to my mother: he was a generous man, bringing home the priciest foods, and updating his car and their furniture every year. But he never hesitated to remind you of his generosity—he'd scarcely miss an opportunity to tell you how much it had cost to invite you to a restaurant, or quote the price of the gift he might someday ask you to give back.

No one knows exactly why they divorced, but I'll share the different stories of how we were separated from our mother. According to my father's sister, my mother composed and signed an abdication of her rights to her two daughters. She abandoned us the day Yara and I left Beirut, and didn't come back to the house so she wouldn't have to see us. My father boasts of another version of the tale, one in which he pointed his assault rifle at my mother's head and forced her to sign us away before sending us to a Palestinian family's home in southern Lebanon until my aunt came to take us with her to Amman. What's strange is that my mother never mentioned this story until I relayed it to her. She remembers nothing of the torments her mother says my father made her endure, except when someone other than me brings them up. I haven't seen this abdication my mother is said to have written, which my aunt would rant about for days on end, hinting that it might be in the Mackintosh tin on the top shelf of her wardrobe, a tin that supposedly contained many a secret document archiving my aunt's private life.

My own firsthand memories belong to another, completely different time. In those days I slept in my aunt's living room on a sofa bed I shared with Yara. To watch Ra'fat al-Hajjan on the Jordanian state TV channel, I would sneak a look through a rip in the blanket, one that grew wider every day thanks to my little fingers. More often than not, I'd eventually feel my aunt's flying slipper hit my head. Then I would sulk to the far side of the sofa, picking up where I'd left off scraping the cracked paint on the wall. That's when I'd start my nightly struggle with Yara's foot. From the other side of the sofa, she would kick at my tummy, usually by mistake, sometimes on purpose.

I couldn't fall asleep if I was hungry, and I couldn't exactly ask my aunt for more food. When she did feed me, it was most often a quarter of a loaf of bread and a tomato, but only if she decided that I was indeed actually hungry. She was usually of the opinion that I was not.

In those days my father was a voice arriving from Spain by telephone. He called almost every month and his calls turned the mood in the house upside down. If he didn't call when he was supposed to, my aunt would turn unbearably volatile. If several days passed without the awaited phone call, she would haul us to the PLO offices in Jabal al-Hussein. We would get into the shared taxi and she'd put me on her lap to avoid paying for the additional seat. There would always be a fight with the driver over the eight piastres she'd have to pay for Yara, at which point we'd continue the journey on foot as she cursed our father and the driver and the day she was brought into this world and everything else. We'd reach the Munazzameh's office and the bald man standing guard at the door would ask: "What? Abu al-Saeed hasn't called?" She'd retell the same story then ask about a man called Abu al-Hol, who was usually not in that day. She'd then drag us in to see the other man, the one they call Abu al-'Enein, tall and dark with a head of thick grey hair. Abu al-'Enein would greet us warmly and tell us, like every other time, how he was a friend of our dad's from the Beirut days, and how he knew our mother and us from when we lived in Hamra. Then he'd remind Yara how he used to drive her to the Rosary Sisters' nursery in his car and she'd scream because she didn't want to go to school. My aunt had little patience for these stories, interrupting him to tell her own, the same one she told to anyone and everyone she'd met for the first or hundredth time:

"This one," she'd say pointing at me, "I have raised since she was nine months old. That one," now pointing to Yara, who'd curl her tongue when she was upset, "was three years old. He sends me only 200 dollars. How am I supposed to take care of them with that?"

She would dry her sweat, moving her hand in a circle around her face, and then adjust the grey headscarf she'd tied the Damascene way to display the front strands of her hennaed hair. I would look at her from my perch on the chair, its leather making my dress ride up and stick to my skin. My eyes would fixate on her two plump legs, each partitioned by the elastic of her nylon stockings, one with a run down the side, barely holding together with the help of Suha's pink nail polish. Abu al-'Enein rarely bothered to feign interest until my aunt slid in the sly coda to her lament: "He's running around after the ladies and leaving his young daughters with me. I have young men in the house!" That last phrase was a calculated call to arms, which anyone and everyone was obliged to take up immediately and without hesitation. We would leave the Munazzameh's office after Abu al-'Enein would give his rote promises to make some calls.

We'd walk around Jabal al-Hussein, eyeing the large window displays. We held on to my aunt's clammy hands, which squeezed and relaxed to the rhythm of pedestrian congestion. We'd walk past the vendors selling ice cream cones, and sometimes my aunt would buy us a cone or a falafel sandwich after haggling with the proprietor over the price of half a loaf of bread. The walk would culminate in a visit to the hair salon where my cousin Suha worked.

One time we were particularly looking forward to the walk after our trip to the office. On our previous visit the salon owner, Um Johnny, had taken Yara to a big shop nearby and bought her a box of chocolate-stuffed biscuits and a bunch of other treats. So this time we entered the salon and immediately set about scouring every corner, on the lookout for Um Johnny. Spotting her, we put on our cutest faces and smiled hopefully at the kindly woman for an eternity from our perch on the sofa behind the salon chairs. It was tricky because we couldn't let our aunt catch us in the act. But Um Johnny was busy with the most peculiar jungle of hair on a customer's head. The salon owner held her breath and avoided looking at the mirror while she battled the wild tufts. The woman in the chair scowled, a look of disgust much like the one my aunt's eldest son would put on when he didn't like what she'd made for dinner, a look that sparked battles that could last until dawn. We put all our energy into waiting for Um Johnny to notice us. She didn't. When she finally realized my aunt was there, she hurriedly greeted her and asked Suha's colleague Khitam to fetch the 50 dinars from the desk. We said our goodbyes after my aunt brusquely pulled Suha's blouse above her collarbone, and returned home carrying nothing but our disappointment.

My father called two days later, announcing that he'd sent the money. My aunt's mood improved immediately. Her smile came back.

I cannot turn my father's voice into features. He is a man made of sound. I'm supposed to be very polite and formal when I speak to him, but I have to call him Baba. It's confusing because my aunt's husband is Baba as well. After all, he does all the things that fathers do. He brings me cream-filled biscuits from the candy factory where he works. Every evening at seven I wait for him to get home, looking out the window in the small door. When he appears, I watch him descend the hill across from the house, his hands behind his hunched back, wearing khakis in the summer, or military fatigues and the black-and-white kufiyyeh on colder days. As soon as I spot him I zero in on his hands, waiting for the moment he'll use them to keep his balance as he navigates the steeper and more slippery stretches. I'm so excited to see what he's brought me. One time it's a telephone that becomes a car you drag by the handset. Another time it's a handbag, and yet another, a doll that yelps "waah" when flipped on its belly.

At night he puts me on his lap and leaves me to play with the holes in his white undershirt, which I diligently widen as he repeats his classic question: "Should I get you a small deery-deer?" To which I give my classic response: "Yes, Baba!"

Whenever my aunt is off visiting one of the neighbors and my uncle returns from work before she does, he goes to the kitchen and makes the most delicious tahina salad, mixing in yogurt and shatta to make his favorite dish. I toast bread on the stove's open flame until it's crisped black around the edges. Then we sit with Yara and Mazen around the small green-and-white patterned table, which we place in front of his special chair in the living room. We race to finish the food, then very carefully clean and wash everything and sit innocently to wait for my aunt to come home. As soon as she enters the house, she swirls her nose around before scuffling into the kitchen. Hearts plunge down into groins as she carries out her meticulous inspection of the rubbish bin, the pantry, and the refrigerator, emerging with an incriminating bottle of olive oil pointed straight at her husband.

"You finished the bottle! Do you have to drown the salad in oil? You know I already cooked, why didn't you have what I made for dinner?"

"What?" he'd retort. "Since when can you sniff things out like a bloodhound?"

The battle commences. My aunt curses the day she, a city girl, married a refugee. He retaliates by reminding her of the cheap flip-flops she wore when he first saw her at her sister's house in the Old City in Nablus. The fight doesn't end until my eldest cousin returns at around ten or eleven at night.

Mazen, my youngest cousin, shares in the covert culinary operations we carry out with my uncle, but Mazen is always angry. According to Suha, his popularity in the family has been on the decline since Yara and I moved in. That's why he rings his hands around my neck the whole way when we go to buy a plate of hummus from the fūl vendor Abu Ahmad, easing his grip when I scream, only to tighten it again when I stop. He is a full ten years older than Yara, but the troubles between them feel somehow ageless.

Mazen's head is full of grey hair. My aunt says his hair changed color after the fright he got when the Jordanian army stormed the house as they hunted for my uncle Faisal during the September War. I wasn't around then, but my aunt describes it as a big battle between the Palestinians and the Jordanians, and that's why we're not supposed to say anything at school about my uncle Faisal or my father's work. Miss Fatima, my schoolteacher, was from al-Tafila and was a "Jordanian-Jordanian," as my aunt described her. Miss Fatima made me memorize poetry and recite it in front of the inspectors from the Ministry. I'd been the school poet since kindergarten. I'm not quite sure how it happened, but I remember that the first poem I read in public was one I'd written in the bathroom. It was at a Mother's Day celebration at Yara's school, which would later become my school as well. My aunt had introduced me to the teachers as someone who could perform a poem about mothers, and suddenly I was on stage. Someone had placed a chair in front of the microphone so I could reach it; I climbed up and began reading. I don't remember my words, but I will never forget the tears they brought to the eyes of the women listening. They whispered as they pointed at me. I heard one say, "Her mother died in the war in Lebanon." After I stepped off the stage, everyone in the hall swarmed me with kisses and chocolate treats. That day I returned home happy. That celebration was the loveliest thing that had ever happened to me, ever.

From that day on, I knew the effect words could have, and their power to usher me into the proud embraces of Miss Fatima and Sitt Zainab, the school principal, after every recital. My teachers seemed astounded by my ability to express myself this way, on stage and on the school's intercom. I'd found a trick that helped me more than anything else: I paced in circles around the rug in the back room, inventing and memorizing new poems with which to wow them.

My father first visited us in Amman when I was six. Naturally, I behaved like any girl seeing her father for the first time. It was summertime, and my father was waiting on the living room sofa that was also my bed. No one knew he'd be able to enter Amman. My aunt had said he was an unwelcome person in Jordan, that if he did try to get in then Jordanian intelligence would put him in jail, that's what they do to anyone involved in Black September. This was the September in which my uncle Faisal was martyred, a framed photograph of him hung in the guest room. All of this was why my father didn't tell anyone he was coming.

"This is your father," they said. So I cried, I was full of joy, I behaved the way I was supposed to behave.

My father was starting on his seventh ice cream cone. He'd crammed ten others into the freezer in my aunt's living room beside the sofa that was my bed. When he hugged me, his smell was overpowering, unlike anything I'd smelled before. He wasn't tall like my other father. He had a little belly that protruded from his torso and sparse wisps of hair above his forehead. His teeth bulged when he munched on the chocolate-coated Eskimo cone, something I'd never tried but immediately coveted. He saw my hungry looks and gave me one. That day I discovered the joy of those ice cream cones, the upside-down solid chocolate pyramid at the bottom. I sat beside him on the sofa, his arm wrapped around me as he told my aunt about his interrogation by the mukhabarat agents at the airport, and how he'd have to report to the intelligence directorate the next day because they'd kept his passport. He was animated as he spoke, squeezing my neck. I wanted to push him away, but his arm was heavy and strong. And I didn't dare.

His presence changed everything. Everyone became exceptionally pleasant, and Yara and I became high-ranking officials in the house. I was happy and excited about what was happening: lots of food, and an aunt whose voice had lost its usual threatening edge.

At night, as always, I left the bathroom still feeling my usual hemorrhoid pains, and went to sit in my uncle's lap. My father yelled at me with his bellowing voice, and almost hit me as he shouted that he was my father and this was my aunt's husband, and he would shoot me if I called that man Baba ever again.

My father—or "The Ice Cream Monster," as Yara and I came to call him—spent fifteen days in Amman aiming to marry a flight attendant called Mariam. Suha had introduced them. When we visited Mariam at her parents' house in Jabal Amman, she joyfully carried me and Yara off to meet her countless sisters. "These are my daughters," she declared, and gave me an expensive chocolate-coated caramel. Another time, when we walked through the market, she bought me a box of chocolate fingers that you dip into a soft chocolate square with mouthwatering results. The box cost 25 piastres, just about the price of twelve days of self-starvation I'd have to suffer if I wanted to buy it myself.

The daily allowance my aunt gave us was two and a half piastres each, which would barely get you half a small falafel sandwich. I'd wait for Yara at the school staircase to combine our allowances into the five piastres that would buy us a falafel sandwich to share. That little morsel was rarely enough for either of our grumbling bellies. I craved the foods in the other girls' lunchboxes: crunchy crisps, sweet cold juices, delectable sandwiches. I often asked my friend Noor to share some of what her mother had packed for her lunch—until Noor finally complained to Miss Fatima, leaving me forever embarrassed. After that, the girls started to hide their food when they saw me.

I associated my father with all things delicious: restaurants, ice cream, a larger allowance. I'll never forget the time the school principal called my aunt to ask if I had stolen the ten piastres my father had given me that morning. My aunt secretly commanded me to spend no more than half of it and bring her back the rest.

My father's involvement with Mariam didn't get any further than the engagement. All I know is that when he suddenly decided to leave her, my aunt inaugurated another mantra: "those flight bitches are whores." In one of their many fights, my father told my aunt that she and her jealousies were to blame. This enraged her. It was his own damned fault for always falling for whores, she yelled, mentioning my mother several times in stories I had no way to understand.

My aunt retrieved the engagement jewelry from Mariam, including a thick heavy gold bracelet that my aunt then wore on special occasions. My father went back to Spain, never to mention Mariam again.

My father was no longer made of sound. He was now associated with several scenes that played in my mind whenever I thought of him: the snores that reverberated into the neighbors' houses, the nap after lunch, the restaurant called Toledo, ice cream. That he was the brother of the aunt I called Mama made things a little less muddled in my head. She was not my mother, and this made me happy. I wanted to tell everyone in the street that this was my aunt and not my mother, and that despite anything she said, I couldn't possibly look like her.

After my father left I began to hear rumors about my mother. The main story that started to flutter on different lips was that she'd died during "the events" in Lebanon. That's what my aunt told my teachers. She also sternly told me never to tell anyone about my father's work. If asked I was to say, "He works for a company." But if the interrogation continued, "Which company?" I was left without a script. The follow-up question would strike me idiotically silent. This responsibility, and the mystery that came with it, were a burden, and it didn't help that it made me the talk of every student at school. At the beginning of each year, teachers would ask students in turn to tell the class about their parents' backgrounds and jobs. When my turn came, I never knew what I was supposed to say about my mother. My first impulse was always to announce that my aunt was not my mother, but if my aunt heard about that she'd most definitely hit me. The neighbors' daughters would ask my sister why we didn't have the same surnames as our cousins. All Yara could think to say was that our mother was in Lebanon. But this was a secret, and out of fear of our aunt's keen and prying ears, we only spoke it in whispers.

The clouds of my family story had a silver lining: I finally had a secret, something special that set me apart. Armed with this secret, I started retreating into my cousins' bedroom, for no other purpose than to think. Their room had some privacy. It was separated from the rest of the house by a wide roofless passageway lined with metal containers that brimmed with the cheese and olives my aunts in Palestine brought with them when they visited in the summer. These were stacked alongside begonias, geraniums, and a ficus my aunt tended when she found the time.

If my father was made of sound, my mother was made of rumors and secrets. I was dumbfounded when I first saw a picture of her. Suha had opened my aunt's Mackintosh tin, extracting a small black-and-white photograph. "This is your mother." The woman in the picture was strangely beautiful. She didn't look like either the actresses on TV or the everyday people we saw on the street. But she looked familiar.

This became my second secret, one I shared with Yara and Suha. We opened the tin every Sunday—Suha's day off from the salon—while my aunt was at the market. This was our time, when we could indulge our forbidden vices. We'd drink cocoa—a magnificent discovery we'd made when Suha got a one-dinar bonus at work—and we'd take a puff of a cigarette lit in the yard, or delight in some sweetened powdered milk.

This is how I began to amass secrets, adding more whenever I could. For seven hours a day I diligently circled the rug in the back room, under the pretense that I was doing my homework or memorizing poems. In my circling I met my mother hundreds of times. I would cry, she would cry, everyone would cry, all from the emotional immensity of the encounter, in which a moment lasted for hours. Then I'd move on, imagining new scenes—the death of my aunt's husband, or my escape with Yara, or the death of my aunt and our dramatic tribulations at the orphanage where we'd end up. When I learned to write I began to record my thoughts. My secrets, now materialized, had to be preserved in a different way. They were no longer mine alone. They could be taken, I could be held to account. My secrets were now dangerous.

My aunt has three sons and one daughter. The middle son we saw on summer vacations, when he'd come home from Damascus laden with braided string cheese and chocolates, which my aunt horded in the cupboard under lock and key. The eldest worked at an auto repair shop, and my aunt always accused him of spending all his money on prostitutes and nurses from the Khalidi Hospital. He'd respond that he was the one who covered the household expenses and paid for his brother's Damascene education. This kind of response triggered her anger, and she'd shout something about how the 60 dinars he contributed were a useless drop in the bucket. Suddenly everyone would join in the deafening fracas that drowned out the sound of the kerosene heater we lit on Fridays to warm the water we all used for our weekly bath.

I despised Fridays the way I despised the screaming and shouting that would begin at breakfast and end after lunch, after which some slept and others watched *What the Viewers Want* on Jordanian state TV. It didn't help that when all the cousins were home, I could no longer be alone in the back room. I had to stay where everyone else was.

One Friday, while everyone was watching TV in the living room, I went to the back room for my rug-circling. It wasn't long before I heard someone coming, so I leaped onto the bed and pretended to be asleep. I lay with my chest to the mattress and my face to the wall. It was summertime, and I wore a light dress that flew up when I landed on the bed, baring my thighs.

I heard the closet door open and close several times, then felt something slowly touch me. It began on my legs and crawled upward. I didn't dare look or breathe. At school we sometimes played "doctor," lifting up our skirts for the doctor to give us a shot in our butts—a game we'd always stop as soon as we saw a teacher.

My bottom clenched involuntarily, the muscles drawing in, just as they did when poked by the pencil masquerading as a syringe.

Less than a minute later, my aunt's voice came calling for my eldest cousin. The hand withdrew, and with it the cousin it belonged to. I instantly jumped out of the bed, fixed my dress, and shut the bedroom door, which my aunt insisted always be kept open.

A new secret, but a frightening one. One I will never share with others however many times it repeats itself, whatever the circumstances, whomever the hands.

My secrets began to multiply. There was the secret about Yara and the teacher's son, who stood on the balcony of his house on the hill across the valley of Wadi Haddadah. My sister faced out the little window in the small door for hours, signing with her hands in a language I didn't understand. She'd met him once while she was buying mulukhiya from the trunk of a vegetable seller's car on the lower street. The boy gave her a letter, the first love letter I'd ever seen—bright scented paper covered in vague and incomprehensible words, and a phone number.

I started to share her anticipation and apprehension, as well as her knowledge of the sign language she used to tell him my aunt was out of the house and it was safe to come over. I stood guard at the window of the small door for fear that my aunt might suddenly show up. What the teacher's son did next came as a surprise. He was in high school, Yara in the sixth grade. When he passed the general exams and got into university, his vigil on the balcony, his beautiful love letters, his phone calls, all stopped. Yara cried in the bathroom, in the kitchen, in the back room. She cried until she met another boy, one she met because he followed her on the way to school.

Firas al-Hamadani Elementary was the closest school to Wadi Haddadah, and we would climb Citadel Hill to get there. In summertime the hillside was covered in yellow wildflowers—with the funny name "dog farts"—and the green wheat stems that yellow by summer and the thorn bushes that pricked my feet as I tried to keep up with Yara. She usually left me behind so she could walk ahead with her friend Layla. Yara had graduated to a green school uniform, and I was still in my blue one (which was actually hers from before she started middle school). It embarrassed her to be seen with me.

The boys would follow behind us on the narrow dirt path that crossed the hill. They'd catcall and whistle at us, making gestures and slipping us letters. Yara pretended not to see them—but she'd straighten up and run her hand through her hair, the soft black carré-cut that fell on her face, and then spin her head suddenly to look at them as if none of that had happened. I envied how she ran her fingers through her bangs and flicked them back like a movie star. My hair was never long enough because it was the canvas on which Suha practiced her hairdressing arts. Whenever she thought it had grown out, she'd come up with a new style to try.

Once, one of the boys on the hill lifted the skirt of my school uniform. I cried. Yara's reaction was to pretend I wasn't there, and then tell me off later for foolishly making a show of my feelings on the street.

She didn't look like me in the slightest. Her eyes were different, and so was her hair, her mannerisms, even the way she spoke. Whenever anyone found out we were sisters they'd immediately seem surprised. Then the comparisons would begin: "Yara is less pretty," or "Yara's hair is softer," or "this one barely resembles Iftikar," or "that one looks just like her dad." I hated when this happened. It was embarrassing, and I bore it silently and pretended not to hear.

Yara, who seemed annoyed by everything, used to get in my aunt's face and scream for a rainbow of reasons—if she didn't like her Eid dress, or hated her haircut. I'd try to calm her down by telling her that the dress, or her hair, or whatever it was, looked great. Then I'd recoil in fear as she kept yelling, and my aunt retaliated by flinging slippers or biting down on Yara's forearm.

At this point we'd heard nothing of our mother, except once when an old woman with thick-rimmed glasses came to visit. My aunt had prepared us. She dressed us in our nice clothes from the small Eid and sprayed us with her special jasmine perfume, and she said, "If she asks whether you want to see your mom, tell her: 'We don't want to see her! We don't have a mother!'"

That day my aunt treated me especially well, so I was especially happy. "We don't have a mother, we don't need one!" I screamed at the old woman, mustering all my acting talents for the theatrical role I hoped would get me my aunt's applause.

Strangely, and despite how I barked in her face, the old woman gave me a white chocolate bar with black raisins. I ate half of it right then and there, since my aunt would likely confiscate it later like she'd confiscated the dinar I'd starved for a month to save up, money she used to buy some olive oil.

Many years later, I learned that the old woman was my mother's mother. Sitting with her, after much time had passed, I heard her recount her version of the visit, complete with details of how my aunt kicked her out onto the street with a deluge of curses and obscenities. She told me how my father had received the news of my birth. I was the second girl, and he'd awaited the coming of a son with the patience of Job. My grandmother's words: "He took me to al-Raouché and said, 'I'll dump you in the sea, ya sharmouta. Instead of two whores, now I have three.'"

I know that my father always dreamed of having a son. To him we were nothing more than whores in the making, an eventuality he would delay through whatever means he could. He always said, "If your daughter grows talons, break them." This gem of wisdom encapsulated his particular philosophy of how to raise a girl.

We heard nothing from my father for a full six-month stretch, a half-rotation around the sun in which all of my aunt's trips to PLO offices came to nothing. Finally a rumor reached her ears, the long and short of which was that my father had moved to Tunis and was now engaged to a 22-year-old Lebanese girl.

When she heard this, my aunt lost her mind, feverishly raving for an entire day. I thought we'd never see the man again, but she eventually managed to get a hold of someone who could reach him to say that she was completely serious about not wanting us in her house anymore.

One morning, she dressed my sister in a tightly fitting dress that revealed the two little mounds on her chest. She dragged us to the Wadi Saqra PLO office, where we finally got to see the venerable Abu al-Hol, and told him, "I have young men in the house and these girls have grown! Make him take his girls, and let's get this over with."

Less than a month later we were in Tunis.

Abu al-Saeed

Tunis, 1993

He puts his hand in his pocket and swears, "I have nothing on me but this one dinar," then walks briskly down the corridor. Awni won't let him get away: he wants 100 dinars advanced on his salary. Mahmoud wants 50, Abu Atef 200.

He darts through them like a movie star dodging paparazzi who hurl themselves at him from every corner. At this job, he's learned since he was posted here, he has to empty his pockets before coming to the office, or else he'll have to lie if he finds himself forced to take an oath. Now he can say with all honesty: "I have nothing in my pocket but these coins."

Everyone wants an advance. Mahmoud's wife has just given birth and he needs to cover the expenses, Abu Atef plans to send his wife and children to visit his in-laws in Beirut, Awni wants money to spend on French prostitutes at the Plaza Casino.

He knows their stories so well it's as if he came up with them himself. The same stories get recycled whenever the end of the month approaches. Only the narrators change. He can't give everyone what they want. The monthly budget from the Munazzameh would barely cover a tenth of what they ask for. He'll send up a request for Mahmoud, but the others can make do when their salaries are paid out at month's end.

He reaches his office and calls home. Yara answers. He asks what they're doing, hears the answer, hangs up. He calls again to make sure it isn't busy after she's hung up on her end, then hangs up again before anyone picks up.

At one in the afternoon he stealthily slides the key into the door. He slinks through the dining room foyer. He hears the two girls' voices. He walks toward the voices and they suddenly go quiet. Jumana is sitting on the sofa in the TV room, but before she can utter a "hello" he steals through to find Yara. She is not in the bedroom. He hears the toilet flush, and when he tries the bathroom door he finds it locked.

"What are you doing?" he booms, still wrestling with the door, which opens to let out the dark-skinned girl.

"I'm peeing!"

"And why did you lock the door?"

She's not sure how to answer.

He walks in to inspect the bathroom. His inquisitive eyes peer behind the sink, into the toilet bowl, onto the window's outer ledge. When he doesn't find anything, he stares at the girl, who's still standing by the door.

"I'll hang you from the ceiling if you lock it again."

"Fine," she responds, her eyes firmly locked on his.

He knows how similar she is to him. "Spiteful brat." Despite all his efforts to tame her, he can't wipe that impudent look from her eyes. Unlike Jumana, who trembles at the sight of him. From the day the two of them showed up to live with him in Tunis, he's made sure they felt they were under constant surveillance, that he could pounce on them at any second. He wants them to be wary, always, even when he's not home. Otherwise he'll lose control over their every action.

He goes into his room and peels off his white shirt and the sweat that drenched it on the trip home from the office. The navy blue trousers, undershirt, and briefs follow. He heaps them onto the floor and slips into his faded green shorts. Everything about him feels groggy. He wishes he could just throw himself on the bed to sleep away the sweltering day until the sun rises on the next.

Jumana follows him to the kitchen in silence. Yara, now outstretched on the sofa, has replaced her in front of the television.

He tries to remember the recipes dictated over the phone by his sister Sameera, his sister-in-law Zahira, and his mother's cousin Muntaha. When his memory fails he calls one of them, who will invariably give a divergent description of what goes into the dish. Regardless, the recipes they give him over the phone lack his mother's masterful touch.

If he calls when the women are visiting a neighbor, the children will call out to their mothers, "It's uncle! Uncle is on the phone." This prompts whichever one it is to rush back to take this all-important call from the absent beloved they only interact with via telephone receiver. The very fact of the call means that he has chosen her, and only her, over all the others.

The kids, for their part, only know this uncle by voice. Still, they carry countless fantastical images of him in their minds. Their mothers remember a dashing young man with soft black hair and a slim body—one who every Eid had the town's only tailor, Abu Salem, fit him with a new suit like whatever Abdel Halim Hafez had worn in the latest of his movies, screened on Friday in the town's only cinema. The whole town spent the week looking forward to watching the film. He was the one who had traveled the world—none of them had ever left Nablus, except the few who'd visited Iftikar in Amman.

He hears the sound of slippers shooting across the floor at breakneck speed to reach the phone lest she cost him one dinar too many.

He sautés the chicken in oil, then pours in water with an onion, cardamom, and a bay leaf just as Sameera instructed. Jumana stands beside the kitchen sink following his orders to peel garlic. She then dices the tomato she forgot to wash for the salad. He asks if she washed it, and when the words refuse to come out of her mouth, he whacks her on the head with the wooden chopping board.

Useless pestilence—she is the wellspring of cholera in the house. Such childlike features, they give her an aura of foolishness. And those eyes. Unresponsively staring off, like the eyes of a sorceress. She could break the plate in his hand or make the tray fall to the kitchen floor just by willing it. She wears a yellow plastic hairband that glows in the dark, and those yellow shorts that annoy him. Everything she brought with her from Amman inflames his disgust; in them he can smell Wadi Haddadah, Iftikar's poverty, her venomous words.

The other one is clear; he knows when she lies, when she pretends, and when her words are honest. This one he knows nothing of except that cursed stare. When he took her to the doctor for the chronic pain in her side, the diagnosis was that the ailment was psychosomatic. It was enough to make him despise her all the more.

"Psychological condition." What does that even mean? He's trying to be a father and a mother at the same time. He's the one who has foregone remarriage for the past fifteen years to raise them. He's the one who moved from Spain to Tunisia to be able to take them from Iftikar. Psychological problem indeed. It was a long trip home from the dark-skinned Tunisian woman doctor's clinic for the dumb-looking girl with the psychological problem.

He puts the finishing touches on the potato stew while the eldest sets the table. He tastes the food, knowing already that it is tasteless, but both girls will have to lick their plates clean. It's not enough that Iftikar has left them with bad manners, they're skinny too.

He fills each of their bowls to the brim, then joins them at the table. They eat as if against their will, but without the slightest objection. He does more monitoring than eating. He knows that as soon as his back is turned they'll dump the food somewhere. Maybe it's the balcony, he hears the cats meowing there every day around this time. Tiring of his surveillance duties, he retreats to the living room for a smoke. There's nothing quite like a cigarette after a meal. "Sacrosanct!" he proclaims to himself as he stuffs a thick Dunhill between his meaty lips and lets his body droop down onto the sofa imported from America. Even as he hears plates clattering in the kitchen, announcing that dinner has likely ended up in the garbage, he does nothing but surrender to the drug.

Afterwards, he goes into his bedroom for his sacred nap, the one that stretches from three o'clock to six. The nap is governed by ironclad rules that he has etched into the girls' heads: all sound is forbidden, waking him is forbidden, letting the phone ring is forbidden, answering the phone is forbidden.

The house is suddenly silent, rhythmically pierced by his snores. By now thoroughly habituated, the girls also sleep. The boredom of the summer holiday leaves them no option but to slumber the time away.

When he wakes, the girls remain in their beds, completely still. He knows the younger one is pretending; her eyelids are clenched. The older one really is asleep. He moves to the living room after serving himself two scoops of ice cream. He splays himself out on the sofa, propping his head up on a pillow to watch an episode of *Mission: Impossible* on M6, dubbed in the French he does not understand.

Abu Atef calls to tell him the card game starts in half an hour. He gets ready to leave, and the girls' reign resumes.

If he were a bit taller, he could have been head of the division. A bit more hair and a bit less belly would also help. These are the only real differences between him and the current director. The college degree isn't important. No one could fault him for having to leave the sixth grade to join the fida'iyyin—even if he did actually drop out well before that to apprentice with the electrician, Salah al-Ju'ba, for a whole dinar every month. If anyone cast suspicions on his education, he could confidently respond that he was a graduate of the Anshas military academy in Algeria, where he trained before the fighters' exodus from Lebanon. Not to mention that completing the sixth grade in his day was the equivalent of high school today. If it were not for the diminutive stature he'd inherited from the father he'd never met, he'd hold a substantially different rank.

Abu Atef was a friend of his brother Faisal in Amman. Faisal was tall. No one knew how he had reached such an altitude, considering the genes of the rest of the fifteen-child family. Their father had all of his children through his two wives, Fatema and Tafida, only to die of a stroke at 40—a health hazard most of his progeny would inherit. He and Faisal shared Fatema as a mother, she was 27 and carrying him in her womb when their father died.

He did not walk until the age of three. One day, Sameera and Iftikar heard someone tell Fatema "Your son is a cripple," so the sisters placed him in a basket they took around to the houses and the shops on the way to the onion market singing "Feed the cripple so he can walk." People gave, and in the basket he was joined by a cucumber, a piece of baklava, sugar-coated chickpeas, white cheese, and tamriyyeh. He ate it all before the girls could find a secluded corner to divvy up their spoils. Over time he got fatter and his chance of walking got slimmer. He doesn't remember any of this, but Iftikar—three years his elder—reminds him of it every time she sees him. He remembers a similar story, but one that took place during Eid. Groups of neighborhood kids would scatter throughout the old city on the first night of the festivities, hopping between doorsteps and shopfronts holding out cloth bags handsewn by their mothers to be filled with sweets and snacks and, if they were lucky, some money.

He grew into a slender young man with soft black hair, and the young women of Ein al-Hilweh camp would line up for a glimpse of him during reveille. He was a first lieutenant, commanding an infantry company at only 20 years old. His promotion was mostly due to chance: Faisal's martyrdom gave him two stars on his epaulette. Otherwise he would have remained a lowly soldier for much longer. But he'd proved himself capable as a commander, skilled in combat, reconnaissance, and interrogation.

Abu Atef is the only one who knows the story of how he got his two stars. He's the only one who knew Faisal when he was a shock-troop commander in Jordan. Faisal was a Tae Kwan Do champion and trained the first waves of fida'iyyin who flocked from the other side of the river, and everywhere else, to Amman, where they trained as guerrillas. He'd also helped set up the staging bases near Nablus, quartering himself there in the woodlands to train the young and eager volunteers.

He never knew Faisal as a brother; he only heard of this sibling through his mother's lamentations. He despised this absent brother, the only person his mother thought about, even though it was he, the living son, who placed a half dinar in her pocket every month while the absent son sent nothing. Even after he fled to Jordan and joined el-Munazzameh, he saw his brother only a few times in the training camps, and mostly from a distance. And there was the time they saw each other at Iftikar's house in Wadi Haddadah. They had a fight about his hair, which Faisal said made him look like a lowlife hippie. That night the Jordanians stormed Iftikar's house looking for Faisal, but Faisal had already left.

He could have been a renowned electrician. He excelled at wiring and lighting homes and shops, and this could have made him rich, a man of capital like his friends Naji al-Aloul and Yasser al-Masri, who never paused before ordering off the café menu, forcing him to order just as fast.

Abu Atef shuffles the two decks and deals, fourteen cards to each of the four players. Often it's Abu al-Nasr who beats them. Majdi wins sometimes, but as for him, he never loses. Abu Atef knows that well, but it doesn't stop him from hosting this card game in the office, to allow some of them time away from their children and from their wives' incessant pleas to go home for the summer holiday or to visit their families in Lebanon or Jordan or Egypt. The men come to escape the headache of it all, or to discuss issues they can't discuss in the morning when the director is in his office—where he'll also be surrounded by supplicants casting aspersions on this one or writing reports on that one, in the hope of getting an advance on their salary without having to go through him as the financial officer.

He knows every one of them. Each of them walks slowly, avoiding eye contact. If the secretary asks what business they hope to discuss, they respond by saying it's a private matter, even though it's never any more than back-fence talk that may or may not lead to the sought-after signature, depending on the boss's mood. After all, the boss also has a wife and children clamoring to spend the holidays elsewhere.

That day, Abu Atef says the words they'd all been waiting for: Um Atef is going to make mulukhiya and bamia stews, and everyone is invited. Abu Atef looks at him and says, "You'll bring the girls, of course."

Um Atef is an original Gazan who knows how to prepare mulukhiya and bamia with garlic and cilantro sauces heavy on the hot chilis. If the mood is right, she might also make tabbuleh and Lebanese-style kubbeh, which is more than anyone can hope for right now.

Abu al-Nasr annoyingly wins that day, but that annoyance is immediately overshadowed by the sight of Awni going up the stairs to the boss's office. He knows exactly what that is about.

Abu Atef cuts the night short at one in the morning. Um Atef is more than likely to punish him with a night on the sofa. It's fine, so long as Um Atef doesn't cancel the dinner invitation, because that's what really matters.

After Iftikar sent the girls to join him, he would have walked in the house at one in the afternoon and not left again until the next morning. But he's grown weary of playing father of the year. The two girls remain strangers, more so than anonymous passersby on the street, despite the year that's passed since they came to live with him. The time for becoming their father has passed, and he doesn't know if he's even capable of caring for creatures of this size. After all, before they arrived, he hadn't taken care of anyone since he was sixteen.

Even though they've never really met their mother, they've inherited everything about her: the loosey-goosey walk, the drawn-out nasal way of speaking, not to mention every feature on their faces. He will do whatever he can to prevent them from becoming carbon copies of their mother and her sister Salma.

He slides the key into the door and merges into the darkness of the house.

He enters the girls' room, the seven bottles of beer he downed making his head spin. He approaches the bed of the youngest. He watches her. She sleeps, no tension wrinkling her eyelids. But the moonlight through the window bounces off her open thighs, chunky and pearly white, nude below her nightshirt. The sight infuriates him, and he resolves to shred the infernal nightshirt come morning.

He enters his own room, rips off his clothes and sleeps naked on the large bed that lacks nothing but a woman. He snores.

With the help of her Tunisian daughter-in-law Munya, Um Atef has set everything out on the table. She has prepared mulukhiya cut finely and coarsely, as well as full-leaf mulukhiya sautéed with shredded chicken and whole garlic cloves the Damascene way. This is the only way Abu al-Nasr eats it. At least there is a consensus in this group on how bamia should be prepared: in tomato sauce with cubed lamb, and she makes that the dining table's centerpiece. Elsewhere on the table she's placed a vat of homemade hummus with tahina— unknown to Tunisians, who know nothing of anything made with tahina. Alongside the hummus are bowls of baba ghannouj and fattoush. No one brings his wife along; these are men-only occasions. He is the only one with the right to bring the girls, and that's because he doesn't have a wife.

Munya takes the two girls into the living room where Maram, Abu Atef's daughter, is watching an episode of *MacGyver* on the French channel M6. Maram goes to a Tunisian school, which means she gets to learn French; the other girls attend the Quds school with its Jordanian curriculum. Maram continues to watch as if they weren't there. She seems annoyed that there are so many men in the house, and mutters her displeasure whenever Um Atef passes in front of her, to which the mother responds with an exaggerated finger-to-mouth shushing. This does not stop the girl's grumbles, "How much more of him and his friends?!"

Yara pays her no mind, and sits with one leg crossed over the other, shaking her foot in the air since her father is not here to forbid the discourtesy. The younger one focuses her energies on not moving at all. She is stuck sitting directly in her father's line of sight, completely exposed to those ever-vigilant eyes on the far end of the guest room beyond the open door.

Maram has long wavy hair and short bangs, which give her face a circular shape like that of the announcer on the television whose hairstyle Yara wants to copy. The sisters eat everything on the plates Um Atef gives them, but Maram does not touch hers. When her mother tells her to eat, she responds, "I told you I wanted to go to the beach today, what a crappy holiday." Her mother quietly shakes her, pleading for her to lower her voice and promising they will go to the pier the next day and do whatever she wants. The youngest follows the conversation intently, saying to herself: *Everything is because she has a mother. If I had a mother my life would be the happiest in the world. If I had a mother I'd tell her that I don't like bamia and prefer mulukhiya. If I had a mother I'd tell her about the blood in my panties. If I had a mother I'd tell her about Yara hitting me this morning. If I had a mother my hair would be wavy and she'd wash it with lemon and olive oil and make it curly. If I had a mother I'd put my feet up on the table and eat popcorn. If I had a mother I'd be the prettiest girl at school.*

After she clears the dishes, Um Atef beckons him over to talk about something in private. Abu Atef joins them a little later. She speaks as if the girls were not in the same room, saying a letter from the girls' grandmother in Beirut had arrived, full of words of longing and pleading to see the two granddaughters. Um Atef is full of compassion, using phrases like "haram, the poor thing." He is silent, smoking a cigarette with his left hand, the other resting on his right knee, his legs spread. The more they hear, the more the girls perk their ears for more. It is the forbidden topic, the one no one ever dares mention. But the finality in his voice is unmistakable, "I am not preventing them from seeing the girls, it's the girls that don't want their mother. Please don't being this up ever again."

He joylessly endures the rest of the luncheon, then sternly summons his daughters. They are the first to leave.

That evening, Yara is determined. Her sister has urged her not to, but she has made up her mind. He sits on the sofa after his sacred nap. He looks relaxed as he watches his French-dubbed episode of *Mission: Impossible*, still not understanding a word. Yara sits on the other end of the sofa, looking at him from time to time, on the brink of uttering the words. Her eyes silently scream, "My life is worth less than shit if I can't say what I want to say right now!"

He knows that look, the one that says she wants to say something she's afraid of saying. He speaks:

"So, what is it?"

"Nothing."

"Speak, I said!"

"Nothing. There's nothing." She smiles knowing this will prod him to keep prodding her.

"I'm the one who knows you," he says, pointing to his genitals: "This is what I brought you out of."

She looks at her sister. Jumana is sitting on the other sofa, her eyebrows pleading for Yara to leave it be. But in the end the words come out.

"I want to get a haircut. I want bangs."

Everything in the room except him gulps.

He sits up straight, knits his eyebrows.

"What?" Overture to the inevitable eruption.

The girl knows she's committed a major infraction. It seems his rage is even worse than usual. How could she have known? His moods shift without anyone knowing the whys and wherefores. No matter, it's too late to retreat, so she steels herself for the advance.

"I want to get bangs."

"You want to make a cuck out of me?"

"What do you mean? I just want to get a haircut, I want bangs."

"No daughter of mine will have bangs!"

"Everyone has them."

"If everyone is a whore, do you want to be a whore too?"

"I'm not a whore."

"Don't you dare talk back."

But the girl doesn't back down. She squats on the sofa, ready for the hand that reaches out to yank her up by her hair. He orders the other girl to fetch the broomstick, an order he often barks out in these situations to scare Yara. Jumana does as she's told, gulping down the lumps bobbing up in her throat. She scurries past him for fear that one of his feet might fly up to kick her. She returns with the wood-handled broom, gingerly placing it beside him on the sofa, but it's Yara who has his full attention. "I'll beat you till this breaks if I hear any more about bangs." But Yara perseveres, crying and clenching her teeth. He commands them to go get all the presents he has ever brought them (a Swatch wristwatch with changeable rubber straps, green Lee Cooper trousers, and a pair of Top-Siders). The little one timidly presents him with these items while Yara seethes in anger on the sofa. He smokes his thick Dunhill cigarette, his right hand resting on his knee. He needs to break the resolve of this impudent, wretched girl who's inherited his infuriating obstinacy.

"A good deed belongs to its doer, a bad one to all." This was the maxim by which both girls would pay for Yara's heinous offense. He beats them to the point of his own exhaustion then drags them to their room. Yara is crying. The younger one tries to console her, but Yara growls at her for being a coward and not speaking up to admit that she too wants bangs.

He leaves the house for the office. On the way, he sees a boy and a girl of Yara's age kissing in front of Le Passage. He walks on, convincing himself he was right, and that he'll have to shorten the leash. If he lets her get the haircut now, then she'll ask to go to Le Passage with her friends, then she'll want to go out with a boy, then she'll become a whore.

He does not want to play cards today.

"She has me all worked up, goddamn her," he confesses to Abu al-Nasr, who responds to the story with a hearty laugh. This only makes him angrier. Abu al-Nasr shares the news that all the girls have bangs these days. His own daughters trim theirs at the kitchen sink every week, with their mother's help, to save money on hairdressing expenses.

When he returns home at two in the morning he goes into the girls' room. To Yara, who is lying with her eyes open, he says, "There's a hair salon on the way to El-Menzah IX, I'll take you tomorrow."

Ecstatically she responds, "She also wants bangs," pointing at her younger sister, who is squeezing her eyelids shut with all her strength.

The next morning, they join him on his way to work. They trail behind him along Nahj al-Hukkam Street, which is lined with small clay villas and embellished with the heady fragrance of jasmine trees from Baghdad and

Damascus that wilt in the summer sun.

The heat is not yet unbearable, and the knowledge that today they'll finally get the haircuts they've wanted makes everything all the more glorious. In Amman a haircut could never have been such a momentous event. Suha practiced on them as she attempted to learn the latest styles demanded by Um Johnny's clientele, so their hair was always short and only began to grow out when they moved to Tunis a year ago. This wouldn't please their aunt Iftikar if she ever found out; she considered long hair inappropriate for little girls, not to mention how inviting it was for lice.

He is also happy. It pains him that he beat Yara over nothing more than some bangs, and now he feels as if he is doing a great deed in making the girls happy, proving to himself that he is indeed the super-dad who has sacrificed all for his daughters' upbringing, who has not married for the past fifteen years for their sake. To further prove the point, after they go to the salon he takes them to the Lebanese restaurant and treats them to a sumptuous breakfast of Arabic bread, mashed fūl, hummus, and falafel.

No one really knows what Tunisians have for breakfast. The reigning theory is that they eat baguettes stuffed with fish stuffed with poached eggs, a theory bolstered by the twin facts that they eat fish at all hours and know nothing of hummus, labaneh, or falafel. It's all rather strange.

The rich breakfast bloats their stomachs and makes him late for work. It doesn't bother him much because he is usually among the first to arrive, which, it follows, gives him the right to be late this once, especially considering the occasion.

In the office the girls feel like VIPs. Everyone spoils them in an attempt to impress him. Abu Ahmad brings them mugs of cinnamon black tea with pistachios. "Don't shake his hand, he'll char you," the super-dad jokes, pointing to Abu Ahmad's black skin. Abu Ahmad and the girls shake hands to spite him. They each let out a different sort of laugh. They sit in his office, where Abu al-Nasr also has a desk facing the window to the garden that surrounds the office building, a white two-story villa with large metallic blue windows and lots of bathrooms. The ground-floor office abounds in pink folders with metallic spines. People come and go constantly. Most of those who come in attempt some form of playful banter with the girls, followed by serious conversations in which the girls are completely ignored. His attitude towards his visitors alternates between gravity and jest, looking serious with his cigarette hanging loosely from his lips, and the occasional puff of authoritative smoke swirling out into the room.

Awni comes in to see him. After greeting the girls and cracking a few unsuccessful jokes about al-Khityar and his fat lips, he produces a piece of paper from his pocket. "Here's a signed memorandum concerning the mission." The paper, signed by the director, authorizes the immediate payment of 500 dollars to its bearer.

"How did you get that, you mudslinger?" he asks, flinging the document down onto his desk.

Awni responds calmly. "Brother Abu al-Saeed, it's a memo and it's signed by the director, that's all there is to it."

He is incensed. He isn't just someone who keeps the key to the safe, someone who buys coffee and tea and disburses salaries and picks out new desks. If he could, he would solve everyone's problems, but here, in his position, with the hard decisions he has to make, he is duty-bound to act on behalf of the souls of the martyrs dying in Palestine, the political captives in the prisons, the refugees in the camps. He is responsible for the funds of the Revolution, even if the boss doesn't appreciate the gravity of the situation.

He didn't struggle his whole life away, face storms of bullets that melted the asphalt on Airport Road in Beirut, live all those years as a foreigner in Spain and Tunisia, just to take orders from this guy. The boss might be a division director now, but back in the day he was just a fresh graduate from the Arab University of Beirut who was under his command in Nahr al-Bared. Back then it was Abu al-Saeed giving the orders.

He informs Awni that he will not authorize the payment. The girls hold on to their seats in fear at the office-shaking clash that ensues, a fight that draws a number of other employees to the office door.

A little while later, Abu Ahmad arrives to summon him to the director's office.

"He's already heard?" he glares suspiciously at Abu Ahmad, who swears on his children's lives that he didn't pass anything on and reminds him that the boss has many eyes, and it's not just Abu Ahmad who circulates news of the goings-on around the building.

It's of no consequence. He rises from his seat, mumbling: "I'll die before I see you get this payment cashed, Awni!"

Abu al-Nasr tries to calm him. "It's between the two of them, man, it's not like it's your father's money."

Angrily, he shoots back, loud enough for the whole office to hear: "It's all-of-us money!" He feels proud for taking his stand, majestic in contrast to Abu al-Nasr's craven spinelessness.

Patriotic songs echo around his head with fervor as he ascends the steps to the director's office, "fida'is- fida'is- fida'is, revolution-revolution of the people" … "I am steadfast-steadfast, I'm steadfast, if they steal my land I'm steadfast" … "I, my brother, I, my sister, I have put my faith in the lost and shackled people, I've picked up the gun so my heirs can pick up the sickle."

He marches to the drumbeats of those songs. Jumana follows, hoping to find a bathroom but not daring to say so for fear of his anger. He doesn't notice her in his long march to the director's office, and, once there, he demands that the secretary make his presence known.

"He's busy," the secretary says, and asks that he take a seat and wait.

"I told you, tell him I'm here," he bellows in the man's face, prompting a voice from behind the door to respond.

"Let him in, let the troublemaker in."

In he goes, and the girl who does not know what else to do trails behind him. She stands at the door where no one notices her.

The director's office is large and he sits behind an imposing desk, with a large black-and-white photograph of Abu Ammar shaking warriors' hands hanging above a mirror on the wall behind him. On brown leather seats beside the desk sit two men with shimmering bald heads and big bellies and a kufiyyeh-clad woman, her hair pulled back neatly like a movie star.

Abu al-Saeed approaches the desk, his stature shrinking with every step into the depths of the voluminous chamber. The director, who looks like Kevin Costner in his role as Whitney Houston's bodyguard, peers at him through large glasses.

"'What's this, Abu al-Saeed? We hear you've been raising your voice."

He stands between the leather seats, the songs in his head fizzling out. "No, I'm not raising my voice," he stammers in a voice the girl has not heard before.

"So what's going on? Why are you shouting in the office?" the director continues, seeming distracted by far more important matters.

He steels himself to speak, the words crowding behind a bottleneck inside him, clamoring to gush forth. *Listen, boy, you're as inconsequential as a puddle, and I haven't forgotten how your legs trembled in fear and you couldn't fight like a man in Lebanon, and now you want to play the macho man and give out missions* and have a coterie of sycophants around you? Not at the expense of the work and the money we send to the families of martyrs and prisoners! In the instant he rehearses this righteous tirade, he catches a glimpse of the girl's reflection in the mirror behind the boss's desk. She is looking right at him—she, the sorceress, who could shatter the mirror right now and blow it up into a hundred fragments, one of which might shoot through the director's neck and obliterate him. But her eyebrows are raised as she peers into his eyes.

She orders him, in a language no one but he could comprehend.

Don't!

"When I get rid of someone, he never comes back. Do you understand that?" the director snorts with a mild crescendo.

Abu al-Saeed looks at him, making eye contact for the first time since entering the office.

"Sir, yes, sir!"

Yara

Tunis, 1993

All he can talk about now is going back to Palestine. He'd rather move to a sewer in Nablus than a palace anywhere else. Not me. I want to stay here, where I can catch a glimpse of Mohammad on the street behind our house or sit next to him in class.

He puts the furniture up for sale, and wants to send us back to my aunt's house in Amman until things are clearer and we return to Palestine. What's strange is that the word "return" doesn't exactly apply to me and Jumana. How do you return somewhere you've never been? I don't understand why we have to feel how everyone wants us to feel. The only things I know about Palestine are what Mr. Khairy, the history teacher, tried to teach us, making us memorize our country's map while threatening us with his shoe. He raged at anyone who mistakenly added a misplaced squiggle to the jagged lines he made us draw and redraw. And there were the newscasts we were forced to watch. Woe unto her who let herself get distracted for even a minute. I suppose you could also add the snippets of conversation about Palestine among the family members who visited my aunt in the summertime, the aunts and cousins who made the already cramped house all the more crowded.

Once again I have to pack my belongings. Once again I have to leave most of them behind. Once again I have to select the crucial from among the important. But I want to bring everything, I don't want to leave anything to anyone. The pictures behind the door I painstakingly clipped from magazines, the schoolbooks I've collected, my old shoes my pillow my bed my sheets. I want them all.

Mohammad says he will also move to Palestine, but we won't be in the same city. Even though we promise to reconnect there, and he writes "I will always love you" on my geography notebook, I know it won't happen. It will be another echo of what happened with Layla, who vanished from my life as soon as we left Amman for Tunis.

I avoid looking my father in the eye as he prepares our egg sandwiches in the kitchen. I place the sandwich in my bag. He doesn't notice I'm there. He hasn't paid attention to anything in a while; he sees us as transient now, as items about to expire. He knows he'll be depositing us at my aunt's house again, and so the exceptionally ample curls of my bangs go unnoticed, although he does make sure to yell at Jumana, who is standing like a statue by the door, waiting for me to join her. Her punishment is in its third day now because of that cursed Latifa. Jumana had heard sounds late at night coming from the living room where Latifa was sleeping. She'd stupidly asked Latifa if my father had woken up in the night. I knew that Latifa slept over sometimes, after a damned thorough cleaning of our home. But how could Jumana ask her such a stupid question?

At school, everyone is talking about the Return. Zainab is thrilled about the prospect and sounds just like my father. She will go to Gaza because that's where her father is. Hanoi, though, will most likely settle in Tulkarem at her grandfather's house, while Linda will head to Beirut with her mother, who won't be going to Palestine because she's opposed to the whole thing. I still don't know what destiny is in store for me and Jumana. My father says he'll go to Gaza, while we'll likely end up with relatives in Nablus, but only after moving back into Aunt Iftikar's house in Amman while he sorts it all out.

Mohammad stands beside Shadi and Fadi on the cement playground. I ignore him, but he waves at me, so I feign surprise at seeing him and wave back. Mr. Muayyad starts the day with his announcements over the intercom: the usual morning exercises, "Attention… at ease… forward, march… about, turn." He then orders Salameh to stand in line with the seventh graders instead of the ninth, but Salameh—record holder for flunking a grade the most times—completely ignores him. The ensuing fistfight between student and teacher is halted by the voice of Mr. Fathi, the principal, who clears his throat to deliver the morning address. This morning's speech is about the Return, about the ecstasy, the elation, and the excitement I do not feel.

Everyone talks about it as if it's inevitable, but I don't believe it. It's just a bad dream, a nightmare I want ended soon.

Mohammad sits beside me in class. I put my schoolbag beside his, between our two chairs. Hanoi jerks at my arm from behind to show me the new magazine she bought at Le Passage with its Whitney Houston centerfold.

Linda opens her math textbook to study for the test in the next period. I should do the same, but no matter how much I study she'll still get a better grade. At least I'm funnier than she is, that's what everybody says. I can make everyone laugh, and everyone wants to talk to me while all she does is study day and night. Perhaps she'll get perfect scores on her general exams and get into medical school. That's what she's always wanted.

I want to study to be a journalist, but I know my father won't allow it. He thinks female reporters are floozies. His plan is for me to become a lawyer. That will never happen.

Zainab and Hanoi usually compete to see who can make the biggest arch with her bangs, who can get her hair to curl the farthest out from her forehead using gel, lemon, and pins. However hard I try to compete, I always fail, first because my hair is much softer than theirs, and second because my father grabs my bangs and ruins them as soon as he notices them on his morning inspections. He generally doesn't notice the rings on my fingers, nor could he know that I undo the top button of the shirt beneath the navy-blue uniform as soon as I reach the school bus. But on this day I was a contender, and my bangs arched out farther than ever before.

Next week is finals and so this is the last week of school in the first semester. After that, no one knows what will happen. These will be the last times I get to slowly place my schoolbag between us so that he touches my hand and tries to hold on to it, while I snap it back as if stung by an electrode.

I don't think I was in love with Mohammad until I knew about this supposed return of ours, even though he's been sending me notes all semester. I like that he's here, and I don't want this feeling of his presence to end. He's not the only one—there are two others, actually three if we want to count the one on the balcony across from our house who I look at from the bedroom window. The other one lives on the top floor of our building, and he has a twin who Jumana thinks about. The third is Mansour in our class's other section. The only thing I share with Mansour is a five-minute glance we exchange at recess. Jumana, obsessed as she is with Mexican soap operas, says that we should not be in love with more than one person at a time. Nevertheless, she and I compete over the number of our suitors and, most of the time, she's the one in the lead. I think Jumana began her adolescence in the fourth grade, before we came to Tunis. Since then she's been unable to be without love. She has an astounding capacity for romance and passion, for bouts of crying, for the kind of longing I never feel. I'm not really affected by things like that. No one can shake me.

But I do love my life here. I've even gotten used to my father's mood swings. He and I are more alike than I'd ever confess. All I know is that I won't let them ruin my life again. My father has to understand this.

My father opens the door to our bedroom. He reeks of alcohol. Jumana is asleep in her bed just a nightstand away. Sheepishly, he says he wants to ask me a question. He seems pitiful in that moment, maybe lonely and in need of a friend. He does that sometimes—he comes and sits beside me, caressing and tickling me in places no one else has touched, then suddenly gets upset, and it's back to the anger.

After two years of living with him in Tunis, I now find him mostly predictable. What worries me at this moment is that I did not close the window. He might see the boy on the balcony, who waved to me just moments before my father came in. My father says he wants to speak to me in the living room. I am terrified for a moment, until I realize that he probably just doesn't want Jumana to overhear.

He sits on the sofa and I remain standing. He pulls a cigarette out of the pack and lights it.

Does he know about Mohammad? Maybe he searched the room while we were at school and discovered the lipstick I'd taped to the bottom of the drawer in the closet. No, if that was it he'd have skipped the formalities. If he knew anything about anything he would have pulverized me already, and this would already be over with.

Several drags into the cigarette, he speaks, saying it all in one go. He says my aunt told him that I'd said my mother used to take us to a man's house when she went to visit my grandmother. His specific question is: did those visits take place before or after she'd given birth to Jumana?

I don't know how to answer this question. On the one hand, this is the first time that he's ever brought up the subject of my mother, and I'm tempted to feel happy to have her existence openly confirmed. On the other hand, I don't remember ever saying anything of the sort to my aunt. If I ever had such a memory, it would have been as a two- or three-year-old. Surely, I would have forgotten all about it in the fourteen years that have passed since then. It seems ridiculous, cruel to invade a three-year-old's memory like this. He takes another drag from the cigarette and commands me to return to my room immediately. I thank God it's over, but he stops me midway.

"Why is the window open?"

"It's hot."

"I said always keep it closed, even if you suffocate."

"Fine."

I lay my head on my pillow, and hear a ruffling from Jumana's bed. I don't dare get close to her because I can still hear my father's feet scuffling outside our door. I turn to face the window, my father's question still galloping around my head.

In my head, Beirut is a river of photographs and flashbacks, its main tributary the photo album in my father's bedside table. We oh-so-carefully opened, poured over, and returned that album to its place almost every time he left the house. I remember my red polka-dot dress, and the photo of me riding a tricycle around the potted plants on the balcony. I remember standing to protect Jumana, not yet a year old, when she was attacked by the tall woman—the one father sent us to, in a car driven by one of his foot-soldiers—because Jumana peed on the woman's orange-striped sheets while the woman was changing her diaper. I remember that Jumana kept crying on the plane while we were flying from Beirut to Amman, and my aunt kept pinching her as if that would stop the cries embarrassing us with the other passengers, and then the flight attendant picked up my infant sister and bounced her in the air until the crying stopped. I wished I'd been the one crying so she'd have picked me up instead. All other tales spring from my aunt's stories, like the one about slime oozing down our faces from our lice-infested scalps "because of your mother's bullshit," and how "the crap your mother took when she was pregnant with Jumana are why your sister's arms and legs are covered with hair and she looks like a gross bushy man."

Why would my father ask me such a question? Does he suspect that Jumana is the daughter of another man? Is she? She doesn't look like me at all. And Suha, who has seen my mother several times, says Jumana doesn't even look like my mother.

I know nothing of my mother. Is she alive or dead? Is she married? Do I have siblings I don't know about? Not a single piece of information about her has reached me from wherever she is. The one time someone asked about us from Lebanon, it was my grandmother, and not the mother who has gone and disappeared. I don't want to see her anyway. I don't want to hear anything about her.

My thoughts veer to the story of Dima, the woman who married my dad's brother. Before completely disappearing on us, she sent my aunt a cassette. She'd apparently also sent copies to her son, then still a toddler, and to others I didn't know. It was a recording of her husband, my uncle, suggesting that she sleep with some men in Saudi Arabia so they could get enough money together to go back to Palestine. Then they could just settle down there for good. The next part of the recording was in Dima's voice, the words clearly meant for her son and for my aunt. In Dima's words, my aunt could finally shut up about how Dima was a shameless slut. She'd divorced my aunt's brother because he'd pimped her out for money, and now everyone could hear the evidence for themselves. To her son she expressed some small relief that at least he'd now know the truth instead of whatever venom my aunt was surely spewing to poison his thoughts.

Before she divorced my uncle, Dima would visit us on her way to see her parents in Jenin. She always brought us the best presents, one for each member of the family. Naturally, my aunt searched Dima's large suitcase whenever she left the house, counting the gifts she meant to take to Jenin, and sometimes pilfering a few for herself.

Dima and Suha would sit in the back room. Jumana and I would sit silently and watch. Dima's presence was wondrous. She had so many stories about men, stories our imaginations could never have conjured. In her stories she could turn men into her playthings, make them do anything and everything she wanted.

She'd slide long slim menthol cigarettes out of the pouch in her handbag. She'd play Ragheb Alama and Rabih el-Khawli, and get up to dance to their songs like Sherihan in those Ramadan riddle shows. She'd slowly unbutton her shirt and slide off her clothes one garment at a time. My sister and I were completely mesmerized. We had no idea how we were supposed to react.

My aunt wouldn't shut up about Dima and my uncle. He'd seemed quite tame and unassuming until we heard their voices on the recording, Dima's describing how she'd forced him to file for divorce with pressure from some of her Saudi acquaintances. He never confirmed nor denied the veracity of the recording, nor did he speak to anyone about the secret behind the divorce, but he was afraid that his application to renew his Saudi residency would be rejected, in which case he'd have to return to Palestine broke and humiliated. He told my aunt that she'd left him with nothing, although she didn't believe a word.

Dima had kept custody of her son, but then she left him with her mother in Jenin when she married a Lebanese man in Saudi Arabia four months and ten days after her divorce. We heard rumors she'd started about herself—that she was a foundling from Beirut picked up by parents from Jenin who raised her. I couldn't figure out the connection between Jenin and Beirut, but I still almost believed it. Suha told us that she'd heard Dima had changed the color of her eyes to blue and put on a Lebanese accent to match her young Lebanese husband.

Dima chose a new story for herself, a story she'd tailored to her needs. I'm afraid that Jumana will do the same someday.

In the morning no one mentions anything. The three of us sit around the kitchen table eating our breakfast with bags under our eyes. Someone knocks at the door. It's Sunday and we don't usually have visitors at this time. My father looks through the peephole and commands us to stay still. He doesn't want to open the door, but the Arabic from the other side is a familiar Tunisian *darija*.

"Open up, Abu al-Saeed. It's Larbi, don't make me call the police."

My father opens the door after Larbi's voice gets louder. He is a skinny and very tall man who greets us daily with a wide grin that shines genuine joy at seeing us. Larbi stands awkwardly by the door telling my father that he can't wait any longer, despite knowing "the situation." Four months have passed since my father last paid rent, the lease will expire at the end of the month, and it can't be renewed without a valid residency permit. So he will have to evict us at the end of the month, and here he is officially informing my father that an appraiser will be coming by this afternoon.

The matter is out of everyone's hands; we all know this. The sight of Larbi's smoldering face that morning says it all, we won't be staying here long. We'll leave no matter how much I want to stay.

That day my father mentions 'Ammo Nur and says he should have done what Nur did and be done with this demeaning life. Three minutes later he takes it back, saying he could never do that. We used to visit 'Ammo Nur's family every Sunday in La Marsa before they vanished suddenly. When he'd told us about their disappearance, my father explained that 'Ammo Nur had emigrated to Sweden and applied for political asylum for himself and his family, never to return. This is how I learned the word *immigration*, a word that means something from which there is no return, especially for people like us. As my father puts it, "if you abandon the cause, it will abandon you." Nur's disappearance came as a shock to everyone, we'd just been at their house two days before and no one had mentioned anything. My father goes off on his now faraway friend, "He has daughters, and raising daughters in European countries is completely unacceptable." We and everyone else feel that 'Ammo Nur ran away. Even though my father has expressed some sympathy, he concludes that it wasn't right. According to 'Ammo Nur's daughter Lubna, they were poorer than we were, even after my father's salary stopped meeting our needs. Lubna said the problems between her parents were constant. I remember one time they fought while we were visiting and 'Ammo Nur, whose gentleness made me want him for a father, almost whacked Auntie Amani with the ashtray.

My father shaves and dresses slowly before leaving the house. From our bedroom Jumana and I count the seconds until he leaves, ready to reoccupy the house and do as we please as soon as the door shuts behind him. We hear the door lock without so much as a whisper from my father. I leave the bedroom to lead the reconnaissance, Jumana bringing up the rear.

As soon as we moved into this place, she and I launched our campaign to ferret out the cameras and surveillance equipment we suspected my father had set up to monitor us from every corner. We've never found anything, but that doesn't stop us from searching. We know he'd intentionally turn over a shoe or place an unassuming hair on the drawer in his bedside table to uncover whatever mischief we're up to. He'd leave the balcony door handle at a certain angle to find out if we'd gone out. What he doesn't know is that we've developed our own counter-measures. Before too long we were really good.

Jumana asks me about the interrogation from the night before.

"I heard him ask if mother saw a man before or after I was born," she presses. I insist that the questions were about the open window. I know she'll turn this into a big deal; she loves playing the victim, the poor girl mired in tragedy, oppressed by all. She loves crying at those tragic cartoons on TV, and I know she sees herself as a real-life Sally. She won't shut up about it and nags me all day. So I pick a fight with her over the T-shirt she wore the day before and how she got chocolate all over it. I'm not sure how it escalates, but soon I find myself pulling her hair and hurling her onto the sofa, while she keeps provoking me with her calculated sobs and her pathetic anguish. Eventually we declare a truce and settle down to watch the weekly Sunday movie on Tunisian television. When we get hungry, Jumana makes a platter of chips that we devour. Within milliseconds there is only one piece left, so we fight over it.

It's been raining all day, so we can't go out on the balcony. I grab the broomstick and give the ceiling a good hard bang. Salim, our Tunisian neighbor upstairs, comes back with two bangs of his own, code for: "Hey." I give the ceiling one bang followed by three others. "We're alone."

My father returns at night. Jumana and I are sitting on the bed, chatting. A putrid stink announces him into our room, its miasma wafting over our beds and up into our nostrils. By the time he steps through the doorway we're already in position, pretending to be asleep, each facing away from the other. He opens the bedroom door, approaches Jumana's bed, shakes her by the shoulder and snarls: "Come."

Jumana follows. No discussion. I can smell her fear blending with the stench he's dragged in with him. He shuts the bedroom door behind him. As soon as I hear the crack of the latch I jump to the closed door and press my ear up against it to listen in on the living room.

I know this slurred speech; those usually-rolled *r*'s transformed into indolent *gh*'s as if he were raised speaking French. He's spoken to her science teacher. He knows she scored a dismal sixteen out of twenty on the test.

"Drop those pants."

I'm not fully in control when I burst through the door and storm the living room. I scream words with no meanings. Jumana stands in the middle of the room in her frilly banana-colored pajamas, and stands up a little straighter when I roar.

"Don't you dare drop anything!"

He is intimidated, suddenly unsure. He explains, as if defending himself, delivering his report, convincing himself of his unassailable righteousness. He is going to spank her for not getting a good grade.

"She will not undress," I hiss, flailing my arms in the air, drawing his ire away from her and provoking him to hit me instead. Our eyes meet at the point of no return, and mine scream he cannot intimidate me, he will do nothing to me. I grab Jumana's hand as if she were a four-year-old and drag her back to the room. He sits back, motionless on the sofa. I shut the bedroom door behind us, and we stand there until we hear him close his own bedroom door.

I hold my sister and we cry into the night.

For him, that night annexes the day that follows. He does not leave his room except to go to the toilet. We hear him heaving in there. Several times we go in to clean up the vomit he's left on the toilet seat.

He deposited us on a plane back to Amman later that week.

Amahl

Beirut, 1979–1982

Daytime had yet to set in when I opened my eyes to his hand roughly poking me in the back.

"Get up!"

Getting up was not something I wanted to do at five in the morning, but his hands kept prodding me in the shoulder.

"You can sleep later."

This man, why can't he be gentle? I thought. I lifted my swollen body by propping myself up on my arms the way our neighbor, Um Fakhri, recommended in her oration on how a pregnant woman should get out of bed. Why doesn't he say "merci" instead of "fine"? Why doesn't he *ahem* before entering the room? Why doesn't he say, "Oh how I love you," instead of, well, nothing at all? Words leave his thick lips with the mundanity of mortar shells.

In those early days my mother would smile away my revulsion. "You'll eventually wear him down."

What she meant to say was, "He'll eventually wear you out."

His version of charming was no better than his default brutishness. Even when he came to charm me the first time we met, in my family's living room in Tariq el-Jdideh, his line was: "The guy who nabs you will be a lucky fella." Everyone has a style when it comes to seduction, I guess, and that was his. Even if I wanted to appreciate the sentiment, I couldn't. His coarse voice, his Palestinian Arabic, my revulsion at the sight of his military boots soiling my mother's carpet—the carpet no one else dared get a speck of dirt on—made his amorous advances fall on my ears like shrapnel crashing through the living room window. His words may as well have been, "May it be God who nabs you, and throws you in a nasty corner of hell."

To be frank, I'd expected nothing different. It started with him coming to our home as a go-between to solve a problem between my uncle Mas'ad and a man from el-Munazzameh. It ended with my mother ordering me to marry him.

If I didn't go willingly, he said, he would just kidnap me and take me as his bride. But he didn't have to waste too much breath. My brother Ahmad, who would never miss an opportunity like this, saw his chance to hit two birds with one stone and stepped in as my suitor's accomplice. An alliance with my PLO paramour would help Ahmad move up the ranks in the Munazzameh, and could pave the way for his marriage to Wafiqa, also a Palestinian from the camp, also a grouch, also disliked by all. Both marriages served Ahmad's opportunism perfectly.

A thorough beating by Ahmad—one he inflicted while our parents were out of the house—that dyed my arms and thighs blue and green for days was followed by a night of torture by Nabila gently applying and savagely removing sugar wax while my mother prepared a glass of lemonade to revive my soul. I was yanked into this new chapter of my life before my pubic hair had a chance to grow back, my mother insisted I be delivered to him still "glimmering" lest he discharge some more of his wrath.

It's not much of a consolation, but she would come to regret her role in all of this.

When we entered our marital home for the first time I knew something horrible was going to happen. I had been somewhat ceremoniously handed over to a ghoul. What masqueraded as our shared intimacy was less than ceremonious: an inexplicable twitch of his hand that grabbed at my face, his lips clasping onto mine, his exhaust pipe of a mouth slobbering its way around. My jaw could have broken, my teeth could have shattered, and I was terrified that he might bite me—but those were kisses, preludes to one body buffeting another, slammed into, jolted. Done.

One night followed another. It was hard labor that we had to perform around the clock until the coming of the heralded Saeed, who disgusted me before he was even conceived. Oh how I hated that son I never carried. I hated the idea of him, his walk, the look in his eyes, the way he ate, the very idea of his existence. Once, as my begetter-half devoured stuffed grape leaves my mother had made so he would appreciate her, I closed my eyes and made myself a secret vow. Saeed would never come to be. Not today. Not any day.

When I first found out that I was pregnant with Yara I knew she was a girl, even though he had forced me to prepare Saeed's blue clothes. He came to accept it, maybe because everyone who saw her said she looked like him, and that the resemblance must be because of the intensity of my love for him. When I gave birth to her I couldn't believe something so hideous could emerge from me: a mass of dark flesh that washed off day by day. He didn't want her at first, but grew somewhat accepting of, almost happy about, her existence. He would return home laden with bags of vegetables, meat, and poultry, the sight of which sent electric shocks all over my body. I had to clean it all. He expected me to de-stem the mulukhiya he brought in by the tens of kilograms in the summer for me to clean and freeze so we could gorge on it all winter. He would dump this load at my feet, then lift Yara to his shoulders and carry her off to the toy store or to Salim's shop, bringing her back with bundles of toys and sweets. When he was out, she waited for him to come home, and maybe she loved him as well.

I liked seeing her with him like that. For fleeting moments I'd feel that I was being unfair. I would list off the qualities of his that I considered good, though I could never quite get beyond what you could count on the fingers of one hand. And it never took long before he erased all of that with a single mood swing.

Today Eid al-Adha begins, and he insists that we have to visit the grave of my aunt's husband in Barja. I can think of no compelling reason for this other than his desire to see Jamal, Nabila's husband, so they can have the rich Eid lunch, competing for the fattiest mincemeat, richest fattet-hummus and greasiest awarmah.

It's difficult getting dressed. None of my clothes really suit or fit me now that I'm in my ninth month. I dress Yara in her Eid clothes as she sleeps. He sits in a chair in the dining room shouting orders to hurry us along. A group of armed men stands below the Cola Bridge beside a field gun. He raises his arm and waves to them and asks about the road to Tariq el-Jdideh.

"It's open," they respond.

If only a missile would strike us right now, this whole thing could be over. Maybe I would be the sole survivor and he would be out of my life forever. It would be best if the incident caused a miscarriage, that way all traces of him would be wiped out. I smile to myself, sliding the thought out of my mind and upbraiding myself for my wicked soul. Still, I replay the daydream on a loop for the entire trip.

We stop at my mother's house to pick her up, as we'd planned the night before. The smells of sheep stomachs and intestines stuffed with rice and mincemeat that she's made especially for the occasion waft all the way from the pots in the apartment to the entrance of the building. Um Sameer sits on a sheet that she's spread out on the floor, a well-worn cutting board between her plump thighs as she rolls grape leaves to go atop the stuffed entrails, adding a whole other layer of toil to the mix.

My mother knows she was supposed to be ready to be picked up so we can head out immediately. She hurriedly changes into her strapless red dress, a choice of outfit that does not augur well for how the day might go.

"I haven't finished preparing the food," she says, like a person who doesn't know that words now have new layers of consequences. "I still have to stuff the stomachs and braise them. I have to make enough for everyone, including all of you."

Before he entered my life, I would never have believed that such a situation could be construed as a serious crime, let alone one that would turn me into the prime culprit. My mother's delay has rubbed the lantern, and the ghoul bursts forth once again, huffing and puffing and cursing and swearing. We're all whores, myself, my mother, my sisters, Yara. When I open my mouth to utter the words, "It's not a big deal," he punches the car's windshield with such force that concentric circles of cracked glass form around the impact. This, of course, only makes him angrier because now he has a windshield that needs replacing. The situation is suddenly more dangerous.

Somehow the day passes and we drive back to our home with me frozen to my seat, trying to rein in my every breath for fear that my oxygen requirements could provoke him. I carry Yara and climb the stairs behind him to the third floor as slowly as my aching back and feet will allow. The electricity is out, adding darkness to the dread in the stairwell. He runs up ahead as if leading a sortie, and leaves the apartment door open. The thought of what lies in wait across its threshold is harrowing.

"This is my house," I tell myself. "I should not have to be afraid to enter my own house," I repeat this as I peer into the living room to see where he might be lurking.

He pounces from the bedroom, holding the Kalashnikov he keeps under our bed. I put Yara down, and she scampers into her room. He grabs at my hair while I'm still in the doorway, and presses the barrel of the rifle against my neck, forcing me down to kneel at his feet.

"I'll drain your blood right here on this doorstep if you ever talk back to me again."

Will he kill me? Would he really? There's nothing to stop him. There's no one who would make him face any repercussions if he did. No one. Ahmad might even kiss his hand and praise him for the deed.

He's going to kill me. He's going to kill me. He's going to kill me.

He doesn't. Ten minutes later he's sitting on the balcony surveying the passersby. He tells me to fry up some mincemeat to layer on top of the hummus he's made. As always, he's used every tool, bowl, and plate we have in the kitchen. Tears are still glimmering on my cheeks, and this annoys him. He takes a break from tormenting the loaf of bread in his hands to glare at me and say, "If you like, I'll beat you for real so these tears don't go to waste."

That was the moment I made the decision on which I would not renege: *I*

*will not stay with this ghoul. I will not stay with this ghoul even if that means killing
him with my own hands.*

Saeed does not come this time either. What comes instead is a plump fair-skinned girl with coarse hair sprouting all over her head. The sight of her strikes me with joy, and him with rage. I can hear him yelling at my mother in the corridor, so can everyone else in the hospital. I try to mute his voice out of my ears and I marvel at this miraculous creature come down to me from the heavens.

This one is really my daughter, I think. She has none of that newborn grime on her, no unseemly rolls of skin, no red blotches. It is as if she'd been born within me months ago, emerging now in all her splendor. He enters my hospital room, despite the nurses pleading and protesting that I am still in childbed, that any anguish I experience could harm the milk in my breasts. I clench my eyelids shut, and my miracle does the same.

"Pretending to be asleep, huh?" he spits. "Of course, the only things you bring into this world are sluts just like you."

He leaves the room and the hospital, dragging my mother with him. He disappears for days. When I get home from the hospital he's not there. He calls several days later. Calm, almost gentle. He was obliged to travel on a mission, he says. He'll be away for a while. He does that sometimes. He asks about the baby, the one whose name he still does not know.

The doctor gave her the name Jumana—Jumana of the ambrosial aroma whisked in dried milk. Um Sameer says, "His voice dried up the milk in your tit, so it doesn't flow." We use powdered milk instead, and Jumana chugs it with zeal.

I take Jumana and move into my father's house. My mother tries everything to convince me not to leave the apartment, but she stops after I threaten to kill myself if anyone forces me to stay. With him away right now, everything is primed and ready. I can finally leave him, especially since Omar is back from Canada. Seeing Omar again, standing beside his mother on the balcony, confirms that all will return to those days Omar and I shared.

Everything seems different in that moment, when Omar smiles at me without his mother noticing. She would not be pleased. She tries to shepherd him back indoors anyway, so he won't see me. The sound of the sardine vendor pushing his cart rises from the street, bringing with it the smell of the sea and the call of "Sardines… Fry 'em up… sardines."

The voices of Milhem Barakat and Georgette Sayegh singing, "Cancel all my appointments, at whatever time you want" blare from the radio my mother positioned on the balcony for all the neighborhood women to hear. Everything feels perfect, until Ahmad's wife Wafiqa storms through the door to tell my mother that she has news to share.

"All hell is going to break loose in Beirut. Israel is going to bomb everything in sight. That's all anyone can talk about in al-Fakhani."

My mother sits across from her on the sofa, looking at me out of the corner of her eye. Our nickname for Wafiqa is "Revolution Radio" because she is privy to all kinds of information about the happenings along the fault lines between West and East Beirut.

"Come, let us see you, Madame Amahl, or are we beneath you now?"

I don't respond, shifting my hips so my bum's directly in her face.

"You should go back to your husband's house already. Enough of this arrogance. The man is pure gold. He hasn't left you wanting for anything, and you stand there on the balcony, on display for all the leering eyes of the neighborhood."

Um Sameer, who doesn't usually like to get dragged into these arguments, puts a stop to my sister-in-law's prodding, expert in the ways of Wafiqa's razor-edged tongue.

"What's with this talk, Wafiqa? Have some shame."

I don't stay quiet either.

"I'm free, habibti. So long as my father is around, I don't owe anybody anything."

"But you're married, Madame Amahl, and your husband is a fida'i who can command the earth to tremble. If he saw you standing out there, half-naked like that, he'd snap your neck."

"Screw you and your fida'iyyin, you ruined the country as soon as you stepped foot in it."

"We're the ones who built Beirut, habibti. The Munazzameh's money splashed here and there is what keeps this country going."

"The Munazzameh can fuck off with its money and theft and depravity and houses shot up like sieves. Just fuck the fuck off already."

Um Sameer came to regret talking back to Wafiqa. That night Ahmad came to the house and tried to beat me right in front of Yara. I have no doubt that I would have ended up in the hospital if my father hadn't intervened and kicked him out, banning him and his wife from entering so long as I'm here.

My father places my head on his tender shoulder, the smell of his familiar cologne and what's left of the black dye he'd rubbed into his hair that morning drifting over my face.

"Don't worry, my girl, I'm here," he whispers.

I know he has no way, no power to stand up to Abu al-Saeed and Ahmad, but in that moment he seems brave, and it's reassuring.

"I've handled Um Sameer all these years, you don't think I can handle that guy?" he chuckles.

We—my father, myself, and Omar's silhouette projected on the curtain across the street—spend that evening on the balcony. He tells me all the stories I know as well as my own name: the story of how Um Sameer, with a face like the moon and hands so milky translucent you could almost see through them, absconded him away from his cousin Sara. News of his engagement to this Sara had traveled far and wide. His family was one of the wealthiest of Mount Lebanon, so the people of the village spoke about it for days. After the engagement he came down with a mysterious illness, one that left him bedridden for many days and nights. Um Sameer was the village nurse and came every day to give him his shot.

"She put her eyes on me," as he put it, "and refused to leave my sickbed until I agreed to elope."

They snuck away to Beirut, where they married. He was ostracized by everyone, and his family cut him off from their fortune. Sara moved to America with her mother to escape the scandalous humiliation.

My father curses himself for those days, somehow certain that Um Sameer had worked some spell that left him unable to have eyes for anyone but her. She was, as she still is, rather homely, unlike him with his famously good looks and elegance.

My father tells this story with pride. It confirms that his fortune would have been different had he not married my mother, that his career as a backup chef at his sister's hotel was nothing more than a wrong turn down destiny's road. But, as with every telling, he ends the story by stressing how happy he was to have all five of us, and emphatically declaring that Um Sameer "isn't all bad." I always felt there was an unsaid continuation to that declaration, something like "even if her looks could never compare to Sara's."

The night is cut short by the sounds of relentless shelling coming from the coast, forcing us to rush indoors. We spend the next days glued to Radio Monte Carlo, with its tales of Abu Ammar bombing Israel in response to the bombing of the south, and of Israelis fleeing Haifa and Tel Aviv for fear of Palestinian rocket fire. Wafiqa comes with snippets of news from the camps, gleefully telling her stories and assuring us that the Americans and the Israelis are begging the Palestinians to silence their artillery fire. At one point, she leans close and whispers into my ear that, though he didn't see her, she has seen Abu al-Saeed wandering through the camp.

I cloak my pendulous postpartum body in a dress that's wide at the waist, and wait for Omar at the main entrance to the Arab University campus. That's where he'd told me to wait when he signaled from the window.

Omar says he won't leave me, but he has to fly away again now in case they shut down the airport. He says his second goodbye, this time to the sound of explosions that stop as suddenly as they'd started, only to suddenly start again.

Abu al-Saeed finally shows up at our door. I hide in the bathroom while Ahmad reluctantly tells him that I want a divorce. My father convinces him it will only be temporary, until I return to my senses. He promises to return me within the three-month waiting period.

"Let's just play along with her divorce shenanigans for now," my father says playfully, my mother serving cold lemonade. Ahmad chimes in as well, promising to beat me until I see stars in the daytime, and to keep beating me until I return to my role as dutiful wife.

He demands to see me, but my father persuades him that I'm afraid, and that he and my mother will treat the two girls as their own until we're reunited. Yara clings to her father's neck, so he takes her out for a spin in his brand-new white Mercedes, bringing her back later that evening.

After long and tiring negotiations, I get my divorce on the condition that he'll get the girls for the whole day every Sunday. That doesn't stop him from sending all his friends to try to get me back. Wafiqa, her mother, and her sister-in-law come with threats, while Muyassar—the wife of his buddy Abu al-Nasr—adopts a more begging-and-pleading approach.

But I have turned to stone, and don't listen to anyone. A strange lightness has unexpectedly taken over my limbs, my body, and my soul. Even Jumana's wails no longer affect me in the same way, especially now that my mother has become so uncharacteristically tender toward the girls since we moved into her house. She's become a mother on my behalf, doing all the things a woman does for her daughters with a delight far beyond my own. I feel that she's much happier turning her large backside to my father, leaving him alone on the balcony to secretly, or openly, flirt with the neighbors while she caresses Jumana or plays house with Yara.

Three months come and go, and nothing happens. Abu al-Saeed passes by every day in a military jeep along with his Kalashnikov-toting friends, and they all stare at the house. My mother, anxious and afraid, desperately slaps herself in the face.

"He'll do it, he'll blow up the building."

Ahmad comforts her, saying he wouldn't dare do anything now, with the Palestinians' situation in the country being as uncertain as it is, as if "on the palm of a goblin," and with such a high likelihood of a full-scale invasion in response to Palestinian artillery fire.

Then comes that Sunday. He stands below, waiting for Ahmad to bring Yara and Jumana down. I look on from behind the flowerpots on my mother's balcony. His mouth hangs open as he shoots me that stare, his eyes have the look I know all too well, and all the fear I've tried to block out since I left him floods in.

I hurry inside unable to reciprocate with a stare of my own. I carefully pack Jumana's bag with diapers, bottles and baby formula, a container of puréed chicken soup, and a spare romper. Yara clamors at me, demanding I paint her mouth with my lipstick. I fear what he'd do to her if I do as she wants, so I usher her out the door as she cries and screams that she doesn't want to go.

I go to Um Abdo, the owner of the clothing store at the top of Corniche al-Mazra'a, to ask for a job.

"She cuts off her own arm and uses it to beg for alms," she sneers to an invisible audience, turning me away. On my way out, I bump into Salma, who doesn't want my mother to spot her because then she'd have to go through all the niceties of a visit to our house. Salma is disgusted by everything to do with Tariq el-Jdideh, and Ahmad and his wife resent her for it. Every time they bump into her or end up visiting the same people during one of the Eids, they fight. Salma mainly shops in Hamra, but she still appreciates Um Abdo's cheap prices on imported clothes, so she drops in when hunting for a bargain.

Salma takes me along in her car to a restaurant overlooking the iconic rocks in the bay at al-Raouché, where the wives of two of her husband's military friends sit at our table waiting for us. As always, Salma makes sure to remind me that under no circumstances am I to bring up anything to do with Tariq el-Jdideh or Abu al-Saeed in their presence.

I'd been to that restaurant with Abu al-Saeed once before. We took his sister and her husband, who were visiting from Amman, as well as my parents. Nothing was spared Iftikar's commentary: nothing was good enough, not the restaurant, not the service, and definitely not the seats, which she spent the evening creatively coming up with ways to describe as uncomfortable. A fight almost broke out between the siblings when Abu al-Saeed decided he'd had enough of her carping. He invited her to return to the haute cuisine restaurants of Wadi Haddadah, which overlook the spectacular rivulet in the valley below her house in Amman. Not one to back down, she released an earth-shattering shriek into his face, violently flailing her arms around and yelling, "Gone are the days of the onion market you crawled out of, huh?! May the Lord protect el-Munazzameh that gave you and your scum the money to squander on your women."

It looked as if she was just getting started, and it would be my turn next, but my mother tactfully changed the subject and diverted her attention to safety. But Iftikar still found opportunities to criticize our surroundings, sulking for the rest of the evening, and ruining it for the rest of us. We finished our food quickly and went home.

He and I couldn't end the night without a vicious fight of our own, which erupted while I was putting Yara to bed. Later I found out from Abu al-Saeed that Iftikar had expected us to offer her and her husband our bedroom, and I pitied her husband for being married to such an ogre.

I don't usually enjoy the company of Salma's friends, but on this particular day I relish it, especially because I haven't been out to a restaurant since leaving Abu al-Saeed. Salma orders meze for the table: tabbuleh, fattoush, kubbeh tartar, liver tartar, and thoom. Her friend Marlene takes over for the mains:

a whole grouper, a platter of shrimp, and calamari for us to share, along with four ice-cold beers.

After lunch we go to a club in Hamra that has taken to opening early for the partygoers. Partying has become too dangerous at night. Someone opens the door from the inside, and we dance to upbeat French songs. Salma hums along as if she knows all the words, though I'm pretty sure she doesn't even speak French. I dance, an image of Omar appearing every time I close my eyes. He'll finish his engineering degree, he'll come back to Beirut, we'll get married. That's what he told me. I didn't ask what would happen to the girls after that, but that can't be allowed to get in the way of actually having a dream come true. His mother would have a heart attack if her son got himself a secondhand family; he is her young handsome engineer, and she's paid everything she has for his first-rate Canadian education.

I'm home by quarter to seven, rushing to make sure I don't run into Abu al-Saeed when he brings the girls home. I get the two mattresses ready beside my bed, and slip into my pajamas. Jumana usually comes back exhausted and soaked in her own tears, while Yara is usually kicking Ahmad and screaming about not wanting to come back.

Ahmad knocks on my bedroom door and asks where I've been. In the matter-of-fact tone one would use to say "there's some food for you in the fridge," he tells me what he's known since four o'clock. Abu al-Saeed brought his sister over from Amman to take the girls back with her, and they are en route through Syria at this very moment.

He grows more flustered as he tries to preempt my response with things like, "Let him take care of his own daughters, our old man has been paying for them for nine whole months already." Realizing the futility of his pathetic attempts to calm my fury, Ahmad reverts to his food-in-the-fridge delivery for the denouement: Abu al-Saeed will return the girls if I return to him.

Ahmad's advice is to go back to my husband and get it over with.

So I killed him.

I killed him. I followed him on the way to the docks. I lost him for a moment, but Abu al-Nasr, thinking I was there to depart with them, pointed me into the crowd. The congestion of bodies and the shower of rice and rose petals buried me alive as I heaved my weight at every fleshy obstacle. I needed to pass through.

All I had done for the past six months was trail him, under the shelling, from base to bunker, from one building to another, begging him to give me back my daughters. Now he was going to board that ship and be gone for good.

There was no way home for the girls, no airport, no safe border crossings, no options. There was only the war.

I stood in front of him and we locked eyes. Women and men I recognized from al-Fakhani swarmed around us. I had to get uncomfortably close before he could hear me ask him to join me away from the crowd. He smelled different, not the expensive smell of the fancy cologne he used to douse himself with. His beard had grown out, and sweat drained down his temples. I begged him to follow me somewhere we could speak and be heard without having to yell. He placed a cigarette between his lips and took a good look into my eyes. Maybe he thought I really was going to board the ship with him. His eyes swelled with tears, no different from all the other eyes crying and shrieking around us. I felt tears in my eyes too, but for different reasons.

He followed me. I could see the emotion welling up inside him. Women pulled at his clothes and shoved their faces and chests into his, kissing and embracing him. He couldn't bear it any longer, compassionately reaching for my hand to drag me out of the fighters' farewell procession that had shut down every street in Beirut.

He walked ahead of me and I followed until we reached a secluded spot on the beach. He looked toward the sea where the waiting ship was docked.

"Where are the girls, Kamal?"

"Come with me. We'll get them and we'll live together."

"Please, Kamal. Give me back my daughters, the poor things will have died at your sister's."

"Even if she has to bury them, so long as you never set eyes on them again."

"I beg you, Kamal, give them back to me."

He was leaving me no choice. I dropped to my knees, my tear-streamed face near his ticklish thighs. But instead of reveling in my supplication he jolted and shoved me to the ground.

"I owe you nothing. And your daughters—you'll see your daughters when I'm dead."

"You're a monster."

He turned and walked along the edge of the sea, his army trousers getting wet and his gait betraying his disappointment. That was the moment to end it all. He had to die. He had to be out of my life and the lives of my daughters for good. His existence was our death. I got up and drew the pistol Ahmad kept hidden in my father's house. Without a word, and just as I'd rehearsed in front of the mirror that morning, I aimed it at him, just as he himself had once taught me, showing off how he could take apart and reassemble a gun in a heartbeat, then placing the gun in my hands. Weight forward, align your target, curl your finger.

Yes, I killed him. His body fell toward the edge of the sea, or maybe that happened after I turned to run away, still holding Ahmad's gun, the gun I told myself wouldn't fire the instant I pulled the trigger.

I ran without looking back. I got to the street, where no one would notice me. The gun was still in my hand, but there were guns in most hands, crying bullets of pride and grief into the air.

I killed him. It wasn't as terrifying as I thought it would be. Every day hundreds died, casualties of a war I had yet to comprehend. His death would affect no one.

I only turned to look back when I reached the street, but I couldn't see his body. Perhaps the sea had taken him far from the coast of Beirut, swallowed him into its depths to feed its fishes. A sudden gust of wind blew into the otherwise breezeless summer day. The wind fanned under my ear, blowing the hair off my neck. It felt as if someone was chasing me, so I ran, away from the boats, away from the cheering crowds, away from the exodus.

I saw the face of Yara mourning her father, and I realized the girls were now orphans: fatherless, after having already been motherless, even though I was right here, still here in this world.

They left on the morning of that last day of August. The television brought us their two-dimensional likenesses, waving from the decks of ships that disappeared into the horizon, salting the sea with their tears. I was struck by sadness, seeing children play with their fathers' assault rifles and mothers crying over what the men had left behind. They had left carrying nothing but, as Wafiqa described it, sailors' bags filled with their most valued possessions. It made me think of our house in Hamra. What had Abu al-Saeed done with our furniture and our things?

I asked around about how to get to Amman. Ahmad said it was impossible; he knew what I was planning. I decided to go to Salma, maybe her husband could help me arrange it. Maybe I could go by land, through Syria. If I got some money together, maybe someone could smuggle me across the border from there.

Wafiqa did not stop crying. Her brother was one of the fighters on the ships, and she'd lost the other in the siege. She kept saying that the Palestinians had been orphaned once again, slapping her cheeks and wailing, "They'll claw us to shreds now that the men are gone." I pitied her. For the first time since I'd met her, her screeching cries did not bother me. I cried with her. I cried and I wailed, and my mother did the same, and so did my father, and so did Ahmad.

Ten days cooped up indoors again. The shelling is intense, the streets empty. News arrives that the Israelis have taken over every street in West Beirut. They are combing the city and its camps for Palestinian fighters.

We pack ourselves into the windowless basement of Ahmad's building. It takes particular effort to put up with Wafiqa slapping her cheeks and screaming her worries. She has lost all means of communicating with her family. We choke on the smell of shit and sweat, blocking our nostrils with pieces of cloth that had been Ahmad's undershirts in a previous life. Water is only for drinking. Food comes from cans that don't require heating. Ahmad and my father do nothing but play backgammon, and we suffer through the shouting matches that follow every game, no matter who wins and who loses. We let Malik and Tania and Ikhlas play with a ball in the hallway between the apartment door and the building's entrance, but they fight, and the hallway becomes the local stadium once the neighbors' children hear the ball bouncing off the wall.

No one can stop Wafiqa leaving after sixteen days below ground. She is determined to head to the camp and bring back her mother, her sister, her sister-in-law, and their children, in case the attack on the camps actually happens, the attack everyone is predicting now that Bashir Gemayel has been assassinated. I too feel I can't stay here a minute longer. I need to know if anyone has found out about Abu al-Saeed, and what I want more than anything is to be outside. Ahmad has to remain in hiding in case they're now arresting Lebanese militants in el-Munazzameh.

I leave with Wafiqa. We cross from Tariq el-Jdideh to the Arab University road without seeing a single car pass by. We see a group of women and children each dragging a drum of water in one hand and bundles of bread in the other. Wafiqa asks them about the road, and they tell her that there are Israeli soldiers at the edge of the camp and on Corniche al-Mazra'a, but that the soldiers aren't blocking anyone who tries to pass. Wafiqa asks me to remind her to get water containers from her mother's house, we can fill them at the well on the way back.

We reach the entrance to the camp. In the distance teams of medics and journalists are moving about. A journalist walks toward us, her shoulders slumped over a camera dangling from her neck beside a card emblazoned with the Swedish flag. She looks distant, devastated, and grabs at the nearest wall to remain upright. I summon my English: "What? What?"

Wafiqa, suddenly speechless, presses her hand to her heart, bracing herself for certain horror. Her only concern is to reach the grocery shop her mother had set up in the middle of the camp after Wafiqa's father passed. The deeper we walk into the camp, the more it smells like a chicken harvester, and the louder the din of the buzzing flies. We near a group walking ahead of us. Wafiqa disappears into their ranks, more agitated with every step. I hear her scream, and scream, and there are foreigners crying, and someone steps out of the group and retches right beside my sandal, and I enter the fray, shoving away those around me to find Wafiqa pulling at her hair, rocking like a pendulum, gaping at a mound of corpses, women, men, and children piled one on top of the other, hands, legs, heads, Wafiqa can make out the tiny head below the sliced open belly of a woman in her forties, "Jana," she screams, "Jana," and she attacks the eviscerated corpse, grabbing the shoulder of a body on top of it and pulling, hurling that body to the ground, and screaming. It was a girl no more than ten years old. Her dress is shredded and I can see everything below her waist. Wafiqa pulls at another body, and then another, but the corpses are weighed down by death. Death a swarm of flies, a greedy murmuration around mouths and ears, crunching at pupils open and glaring from eyes that last saw what cannot be borne.

Jana is somehow pulled out from beneath the pile of neighbors she'd yet to meet. She is, or was, the same age as Jumana—barely a year-and-a-half. Wafiqa's sister Mariam and I had given birth the same week. Wafiqa holds the child to her chest, dried blood and flies covering the infant's face, her head hanging limp off her shoulders like a doll broken in a fight between playmates. Wafiqa carries Jana in her arms and forces her way through the crowd toward her mother's shop.

Women, children, and the elderly are roaming the alleys, searching, like us. At each pile of corpses, we find someone looking for an arm that concerns them. In another mound, we find Jana's mother. We find Jana's brother face down in front of the shop. Wafiqa's mother is the only one who survived. We find her, voiceless, in the corner of Safiyya's classroom in the Agency school.

I begin to visit the school every day with all the food and water my arms can carry. I bring the tins of powdered milk and baby food I had hoarded for Jumana when talk of the war had started. I breastfeed a little girl who refuses the bottle. A woman tells me the baby's mother was about to wean her because she made her nipples bleed. I hold her in my arms, and she looks up at me just as Jumana used to. She pulls at my hair.

I nickname her "Juju." The Agency school residents nickname me "the Palestinian's wife." I've told everyone about my two Palestinian daughters, who are with their aunt in Amman because their father was worried for them, with the war and everything.

"Jumana is in her second year now. She's been walking for some time, and her upper teeth have grown in." I say this to the woman who only wakes up to ask about a boy named Walid. "Juju still wears diapers," I add, "but she'll learn to use the toilet soon. She can't be without her bottle, even if she's eaten a whole pot of rice. Yara is in preparatory school. She speaks English fluently. We'll have to buy her a bigger bicycle next year because she's growing like an ogre.

She's inherited her genes from my brother, Sameer. She's obstinate and won't take no for an answer. Jumana will be more patient. Maybe she'll become a pilot; she likes to play with airplanes. Surely, by the time they're older, this will be a world where girls can fly planes."

Jumana

Jerusalem, 2011

All I really want is soft bedding, with a huggable duvet I can curl up and hide under. Sometimes I wonder why I don't just get out the cheap blanket, instead of bothering with all the hassle of making everything look pretty. Why are newlyweds obliged to get these sets with the matching, but utterly useless, frilly pillowcases? Why not just use the comfy ugly ones? I guess it's so we can pretend to be fancy in case a guest decides to peek into our bedroom.

Thinking back, I did use that cheap cover in the first months of our marriage. Since then I've done what I felt I was supposed to: pointlessly spread the expensive bedcover and its fatuous pillows out every morning and fold it up all over again every evening. It would still only be the two of us who'd see it, whether it was on display in all its glory on the bed, or stuffed between the closet and the nightstand, on top of the risqué nightgowns Yara forced me to buy.

The bed in question is less our bed than it is his bed, and my bed. Each of us has their own special territory where we freely unfurl our limbs, so long as they don't breach the invisible armistice line that the gap between our pillows creates in our minds. His pillow is about twice as long as mine, but neither of us makes much of the fact that his share of the bed is larger, or that borders shouldn't be determined by the arbitrariness of a valley between pillows.

On my side of the border is my pillow. It's actually two down pillows crammed into one pillowcase, with a history that stretches back to my high-school graduation. His pillow, over on the other side, has a lineage that stretches back into the last century. It's long and stuffed with cotton, a hand-me-down from his mother. Her house is full of these battered remains of pillows, with bright yellow or sky-blue satin edges bordering the frayed and yellowed checkerboards of quilted red and brown squares that blend in seamlessly with their discordant surroundings.

Our pillow situation isn't the result of us neglecting to buy modern, luxurious pillows to go with our new bedroom. We actually bought the very best pillows the market had to offer, almost as if to prove that we could afford whatever grade of ergonomic memory-foam our cheeks desired, or whatever was the polar opposite of the mold-and-sweat-stained fabrics of our parents' homes. But those silky, firm pillows brought us nothing but three sleepless nights, cricks in our necks, and the snore-like sounds he produced as he jostled to find a comfortable position for his wakeful head. Ultimately, we had to admit defeat, waving away the white pillows of our surrender, and calling for reinforcements from our premarital pillows to join in the fray of our newlywed ecstasies.

From my vantage point at the far corner of my pillow, the bed appears vast; the frontier between us is a long, rectangular void. In her first months out of my womb, Shireen occupied that gap. She cried throughout the night, so we brought her into our bed, which by then was no longer the arena for much ecstasy. The void transformed; it became a cosmic horror that repelled us as far from it as possible, our bodies tensed in vigilance, lest an involuntary movement render this frightening thing, who deprived us of the mere taste of sleep, into a squished slab of basterma. Those nights dragged on, and we awaited the oft-heralded ceasefire, the one everyone said would come. At first, they said, "Wait until she's 40 days old." But sleep rejected our pleas. "It gets better three months in," they said. We waited six months, then a year, but Shireen defied all predictions with impunity, leaving us to launch our hopes into each following month, bombarding any hope that she'd ever live up to the readymade formulas veteran parents proffer upon rookies like us. I imagined putting her in a cardboard box on the balcony and closing the door behind me so she would cry unheard through the night. I could see myself grasping her in my hands like a teddy bear that I'd slam into the wall and pound with kicks and blows to silence the cries once and forever more.

In truth, none of that happened. In those days I came to understand why Yara compared early motherhood to sleeping on a bed of nails, and certainty dawned on me in ways those early motherhood mornings never did.

I could not be a mother.

I felt like I was playacting the emotions mothers express: the magical feeling that supposedly descends from the heavens when they see their children for the first time. Already, the moment I placed Shireen in the Maqased Hospital's nursery ward with the six groaning women ranting about the godsend of child-subsidy checks, I had no clue how I would be conjoined with this creature over the lifetime to come. The nurse, who hadn't breastfed a child a day in her life, explained how to wipe my nipple and squeeze it between two fingers in order to prepare meals for the baby. "Do it every two hours," she oozed confidently, mentioning nothing about what would happen to this breast, a breast that had been arrogant toward cold in the wintertime and rhapsodic in summertime. No, she didn't mention that after becoming swollen and cracked from repeated suction, it would deflate like a punctured tire after the baby was done with it.

Indeed, I was no mother. Nor was I capable of being one.

Then the magic happened. It was three in the morning, and I was exhausted to the verge of keeling over as I walked, reeled in by Shireen's incessant screams. She was in her fifteenth month. I looked at her, and she reciprocated with a violent, terrifying glare of her own. I bawled, loudly. She stared at me, intrigued. I was doing something that belonged squarely among her own duties. I leaned over the bars of her crib and told her that I was tired and wanted to sleep.

"For God's sake," I pleaded. "Don't cry."

Shireen was silenced, perhaps mortified by my pathetic appearance. She took pity, looking at me out of the corner of her eye and smiling, then granting me leave to go with a wave of her hand.

With all the world's compassion, her eyes said: "Go now, and rest. I won't disturb you."

I couldn't believe her reaction, but I complied meekly, moving slowly for fear that she might change her mind and recommence the wailing that would certainly mean another long and sleepless night. But no. Shireen slept, and I slept, and we became the best of friends.

The bed seems vast now that Shireen is in her own crib far from our nightly battles. I look over at Suheil, who takes off his glasses before going to bed, leaving his eyebrows startlingly thicker, and his face seemingly formless, border-free. He cradles his head in his hands and sleeps quietly. I want to shake him awake to tell him all the thoughts I've been keeping from him, because I think his simple mind—which has no comprehension of what a truly complicated life would look like—wouldn't understand being woken up in the middle of the night to my demand: "Hold me." He would think it unnecessary lunacy. But I'm scared, and the abyss between our two sides of the bed only widens.

The television brings news of earthquakes and floods and revolutions. Death is on offer, on our screens, free of charge. Revolutions everywhere—Tunisia, Egypt, Yemen, Bahrain, Syria. I try to formulate my stance on each of them, but I can't. I want to go out and declare a revolution against something, but I can't. When I analyze the situation with my friend Tania, she tells me that those who have grown accustomed to oppression justify their own as the only way to remain both sane and alive. She mentions a kind of psychological phenomenon through which the oppressed develop feelings of attachment, and even compassion, for their oppressor. But I want to change. I want the courage to take an impassioned stance toward events like these. I turn my eyes away from the footage of a family slaughtered in Syria, only to catch sight of a dusty photograph of my father stowed on the shelf under the TV. It was taken when he retired, and I've never framed it. I remember the day he went to have that portrait taken; it was the only time I saw him in a military uniform. It had been a very long time since he was a military man, but he wanted to be remembered as a fighter. It was as if he wanted to erase the long years he'd spent sitting behind a desk, nothing moving forward in his life but his potbelly. All that was left for him was to exalt in the majesty of the few years he'd spent as a soldier, in a uniform that almost certainly looked nothing like the one in the photograph. He moved his beret around, trying different ways to get it to fit his large head and conceal his baldness. Despite all his efforts to trick the camera, he managed to hide only a small section at the crown of his head.

Since that day four years ago when I found out about the blood-type mismatch, I've come up with several rational explanations. Suheil refuses to entertain any logic grounded in coincidence, sorcery, or the paranormal. The first explanation, the one he champions, is that the wrong blood type may have been recorded on my father's military ID. I don't find that one plausible because my father had several operations in various hospitals, and someone would have caught the error.

The second possibility is that there was a mix-up at the hospital where I was born, and I was accidentally swapped with another baby. Suheil doesn't support this theory, and neither do I because, despite everything else, I do have my mother's brown hair and her dimples.

The third explanation is that I am not my father's daughter, and that I'm maybe the daughter of the man who smiled at me from the picture hanging in my mother's living room, the man who became her husband after she and my father divorced. This would mean that I'm not even Palestinian. Not only would this negate all that my life has been to date, it could seriously complicate my application for family unification so I can get the blue Jerusalem ID card.

The blood-type mismatch could also be a freak mutation of blood cells with no broader meaning, a possibility Suheil finds to be the most logical, but which I find to be a cold dashing of dreams I don't want dashed.

I thought I could resolve the whole thing by having a DNA test performed on a single strand of Yara's hair, but this turned out to be more complicated than I thought. These tests are only done for criminal investigations, or with both parties' consent. Naturally, Yara refuses to even consider the possibility. She's told me not to mention it in front of Suheil because the result could mean I was illegitimate and that could mess up my marriage. The few times she and I have talked about it, she's escalated the conversation into a full-blown fight, as if I'd seriously disrespected her by even thinking any of these questions. Her mouth wouldn't say it, but I could read the words in her enraged eyes: "Why do you want to abandon me? Don't turn your presence in my life into a lie and leave me stranded, alone in my truth." After a while I came to understand Yara's anger. I stopped bringing it up. I felt as if I'd outgrown her when it came to this subject, and this made me sympathize with her. She doesn't have a story that could offer her an alternative, a truth different from the one we had lived. Now, perhaps, I do.

I met my mother for the first time behind my father's back. It was a dramatic reunion that brought us together in Amman. Everyone cried. My mother didn't resemble the only picture of her that I'd seen, the one in my aunt's Mackintosh tin. Instead, she was more compact, her eyes smaller and without the glimmer I vividly recalled. I was engrossed as I watched her coddle Salim, the youngest of the children she'd had with her second husband. I wished I'd had *that* woman as my mother. The second time I saw her was in Beirut. This time my father knew we were meeting. Telling him was easier than I'd imagined. I'd just graduated but couldn't find a job. At that time, I'd come down with all kinds of psychological problems that made my father think I might really die, this time from some kind of inexplicable illness. When I finally gathered all of my courage and told him that I wanted to go see my mother in Beirut, he matter-of-factly responded in the positive. This was of course followed by a long interrogation on how I'd found her number and what we'd said to one another on the phone. I think he wanted to prove that he'd never been opposed to us meeting her, that it was Yara and I who had just never brought it up.

To be honest, I wasn't really going to Beirut to see my mother. My real reason for going was that a man I'd fallen in love with wanted to visit Lebanon. In those days I was a magnet for overly dramatic men, men who made the biggest mountains out of the smallest molehills. This man was the most histrionic of them all. We left for Beirut after my mother helped me arrange an entry visa, and he sat beside me, right there in her house. She didn't seem to mind. He and I spent a week together in Beirut—a week of him hitting on every woman who crossed our path, from the saleswoman at the clothing boutique and the waitress at the café to my oh-so-svelte cousin. He had one particularly dramatic episode when my mother brought up the possibility of us getting married: he got up, completely set on storming out of the house. He didn't leave, of course; it was a piece of theater to get me to beg him not to go, and I delivered my command performance. He spent the week in Beirut with me, and I stayed with my mother for the remainder of the month, a month that felt like the longest in my life. He had left, but I wanted to be with him, he was the only one I wanted to be with. Whether or not my mother was there made no difference.

My mother would leave for work in the mornings and return around midday to take me to the Bain Militaire where we'd meet her friends Rawan 'Addum and Salam Tabbara, who held their lips open in an uncannily identical way. When we were with them, my mother would try to form her lips to do the same. My aunt, the retired general's wife, would also be there, clad in her bright-orange bikini. She would throw her towel over a chair, and plop herself there for many a long hour, her golden sandals at the ready beside her. I was the most boorish girl on the beach, a fact confirmed by my mother's glares at my doughy white thighs. My mother urged me to swim while she admired the slender bodies of her friends' daughters, their hair reaching halfway down their backs.

My aunt handed me a bottle of tanning lotion. "Here, get some color." I didn't use it because I knew my skin would burn the way it had in Tunis whenever I threw myself on the beach without sunscreen like the other girls. Naturally, my mother didn't appreciate me turning down her sister's offer, but her chagrin evaporated when she shifted her attention to a group of women thronged around a man standing in front of us. A woman beside us said that he was a music-video producer and had cast her daughter in a TV ad shot the previous month. Not to be upstaged, my mother took her cue, and jostled her way to the center of the crowd.

"My son, Fadi, is a director. The play he's working on will be premiering soon."

Of course, Fadi hadn't yet finished his theater degree, but he'd be pleased to know his mother had moved on from telling everyone her son was a pilot because he'd once been accepted into the aviation academy.

Salim and Fadi constantly mock and mimic my mom and her friends' exaggerations. They're especially hilarious when it comes to my aunt, the general's wife, whose penchant for plastic surgery make her the butt of many a joke among us cousins. My mother pretends not to have heard any of this commentary, persistently holding firm to the *contrevérités* of her extraordinary stories whenever she's in one of those gatherings of the *tantes*.

Whenever I go to Beirut, I come back wishing I hadn't gone, but I always find reasons to return. I sometimes miss having a mother, the mother I conjured as I circled the rug in my aunt's house, alone and afraid. That mother had nothing to do with the woman I see on my trips to Beirut. The mother I imagined in Amman had broad shoulders, the kind that could cushion a head and fill it with the thousand smells of a day spent in the kitchen. That mother combed through my hair on the house's rooftop on crisp sunny days in winter, plucking one louse after another; she exuded prayers and incense and amulets. She was a mother made of songs. I would miss that mother in the same way that I'd miss the father ready with dirty jokes to lighten the mood of any gathering when a gloom settled in. The dreamy bubble of that longing would pop as soon as I'd remember how my father would dismiss anything I said in front of others, or how he regularly threatened to hang me from the ceiling for absolutely anything I had or hadn't done, no matter how trivial. I used to think that all fathers were like mine, but when I started watching Suheil as he held Shireen, refusing to leave the house in order to stay with her, I felt envious. I wished I'd had a father who was more like my husband.

I wonder what Shireen thinks of me as a mother—a mother who doesn't believe in motherhood. I'm convinced that motherhood is an idea invented for the building of societies, a political and social concept more than a fundamentally human one. It does nothing but discipline and shackle life. Perhaps there is a way to end this. I often feel like dropping everything and just leaving. I'm too weak to stay with these two. That might be why, when Tania brought up a conference being held in the United States to celebrate masturbation—and her gripe with the organizers promoting the conference on the grounds that masturbation is somehow good for health—I didn't find it weird or contemptible. I like the idea that masturbation is good for you. I had no doubt that Tania masturbated almost every day, probably before going to sleep and most likely accompanied by her computer, that conveyor of all delicacies for all appetites.

I don't remember when I became addicted to the websites that offer the full pornographic spectrum. It didn't take long for me to find my favorite genre: scenes depicting women bound and beaten, hanging by their breasts as men thrash them mercilessly, only for these women to appear at the end of the film gushing over how much they enjoyed the experience, anxious for the opportunity to do it again.

I feel more discomfort than excitement while watching these scenes, yet I find myself always returning for more, seeking more—more beating and flogging and humiliation. Yara's husband Majed is also addicted to these websites. According to Yara, most of her fights with Majed are because he's not sexually gratified like the men in the videos he watches. When my father heard about this, he was angry about having a son-in-law who lowered himself to watching smut, but he still commanded Yara to do whatever Majed wanted. This, of course, made Yara furious. My father's defense against Yara's rage was to exaggerate his illness, lying on the sofa with his hands clutched to his chest. But this was futile. She hurled vicious insults at him, at Majed, and at the day she came into this world.

Although it's been four years since our father died, Yara still hasn't gathered the courage to leave Majed. She says it's because of their children, and of what people would say, and because of other things I don't find convincing. Despite her thin veneer as a harsh and stony person who cares only about herself, Yara will not get divorced. The more I push her to leave, the more she insists that she will not let our tragedy repeat itself.

Suheil knows what I'm set on doing, but he doesn't trust any lab that would do the test without official authorization. Yet he doesn't object outright. He says what he always says: "Whatever you want." And although I'd thought the test was all I wanted, I later found out that I couldn't make such decisions on my own, so I just didn't make them. That's why I've quit one job after another, just as I left man after man in the past. Suheil says I avoid confrontation, and that this trait will hold me back and keep me from success. I agree with him because I can't argue back, so he stops the conversation there and says: "Whatever you want."

I wake up to the sound of Shireen screaming: "I want go pee pee." That means she's already done it. All that's left is for me to clean up the crime scene. I force myself up. Suheil is already up, shaving in the bathroom. Without exchanging a word, we commence the crib-cleaning ritual. Shireen gives me a kiss in an attempt at emotional blackmail, which she hopes will spare her my scolding for this—now almost daily—transgression. Next, I move to the kitchen, perplexed as usual about what kind of sandwich to pack for her lunch. I've tried everything: labaneh with black olives, like the sandwiches Sami used to bring to kindergarten when we were kids, sliced smoked meat with white cheese; I've even tried putting wheat flakes in her milk container. The only lunch she wants, she insists, is a boiled-egg baguette.

Yesterday, I tried to get my mother to talk. I sent her a Facebook message asking for a Skype conversation, but the internet connection wasn't strong enough for a video call. So, I used my keyboard, asking her to tell me about my father, about myself when I was a newborn. If only I could get her to talk, then maybe she'd tell me the truth and spare me the ordeal of the shady laboratory. She seemed excited, as if she'd been waiting for someone to ask her to tell her story. Two days later, I open my Messenger to find this:

I asked for a divorce

He agreed after 3 months of negotiations

If Abu al-Saeed agreed to the divorce, Baba promised he'd get us back together within the 3-month waiting period

I was the most beautiful of Beirut's beauties

A face like the moon, red like a rose with velvet cheeks

Two green eyes

You girls and I spent the time at my parents' house, around 6 months

He'd take you and your sister every Sunday

Hoping I'd go back on my decision

But I was the one who'd become "Free and Free and Free" like
Darwish says

I didn't agree to go back to him. He didn't send a single penny for you—
his own children—the whole time I was at my parents' house

He tried to pressure me, many many times

Once he tried to take you to his friend's house in Saida

Sometimes he sent my brother, your uncle Ahmad, to threaten me
with a gun

Then I had a nervous breakdown

He took you every Sunday. Except that Sunday when his sister came
from Amman

He came to take you like every other Sunday, but this time he didn't
bring you back

When I asked him where you were he said "You'll find out when you
come back to me, you'll only get them back if you cancel the divorce."

But have you ever heard of a bird who left the cage and then returned to it?

The price he asked was my freedom

I cried blood, months passed, the Israelis invaded

The Palestinians fought for 3 months, and Beirut was destroyed

Devastation, death, planes dropping bombs on every speck of the city

Until Abu Ammar agreed to leave Lebanon

And after the Palestinian fighters left, there was the brutal war between the Lebanese Forces and the Socialist Party, the War of the Mountain

Beirut's airport was shut down for 2 years

I cried a lot, and thanked God for everything

We stayed in the bunker day and night

My tears didn't give up on the idea that the day would come when I'd be reunited with you

That's when my mother went to Amman, but your aunt ignored her

So she went to the higherups in the Munazzameh… an old friend of hers helped

And she saw you

Finally, my mother's side of the story, but it didn't help. I had to hold myself back from laughing—her texts appeared on my screen beside a photo on her homepage of her posed with a Turkish soap opera star. The relationship between us isn't exactly typical of a mother and daughter, yet I still felt some shame about asking her directly whether she'd cheated on my father and had me by another man. Could he be the one who became her husband later, the one who's now, sadly, deceased? I wouldn't put it past her to do something like this, not because of all the horrible things my aunt has said about her, but because of the incident from my last visit to Beirut.

At that time, I was still pregnant with Shireen. My mother handed me a plastic urine-test container and asked me to fill it. At first I thought she wanted to run some tests to see if everything was fine with my pregnancy. I'd even felt pleased to think that she cared. I later found out that she had been married "unofficially" to a bigamist. She "divorced" him but wanted to convince him that she was pregnant. She took the container of my urine and went straight into her room, forgetting that I existed and that Suheil was sleeping in Salim and Fadi's room right beside us. She broke out into a song by Amr Diab at the top of her lungs, put on a low-cut pink dress, and left. When she came back a little before midnight, I didn't ask where she'd been. She was in a good mood and had brought back gifts for everyone but me. I went into Salim and Fadi's room and choked on my tears as I told Suheil that I never wanted to come back to this house. Suheil felt a similar discomfort, a claustrophobia we would later explain by saying that we live in a different world from my mother, and the two worlds can't collide for more than three days at a time.

Every time I think back to that incident I wonder: why do I want to belong to her world? Why do I want to shake off the long years I've lived on the uncouth side of the cosmos, and belong instead to that softer silkier side, even if it's the cheap mass-produced-in-China silk that makes your skin crawl after a while? I've lived my whole life trying to convince myself that I don't belong to my father. He is undoubtedly not my father. I even overheard him ask Yara about my mother and that man once, which made me indescribably happy. Finally, I could explain why I felt like I didn't belong, and I could prove I was made of something better. But now I don't want to belong to my mother, either.

I wait for the light rail that passes in front of my house. I've made sure to have my green West Bank ID card in the outside pocket of my handbag, to avoid drawing attention when yelled at to produce it. Beside me on the platform stands a thin white woman wearing a blue headscarf tied at the back. In front of her is a stroller with two tiny children, and beside her stand three teen boys and two girls. The boys wear yarmulkes, pinned on the crowns of their heads. Their long sideburns curl down toward their shoulders. The girls wear skirts that look like a school uniform and small round glasses with very thick lenses. The woman asks me something in an elegant-sounding Hebrew. I shake my head, smiling, and confess in English that I don't understand. She says a few more words and walks away with all her children in tow, except for the youngest who stays behind tying his shoelace. Then, from a distance, another woman approaches. She wears a green headscarf, tied at the front. Her pram only bears one infant, but five other children huddle around her, their clothing unconnected by any coherent theme. The two women stand near one another, and the children from each group eye those in the other in what seems like a kind of ritual. The train arrives, and everyone boards, all in one go. I try to sit as far away as I can from both groups.

I conduct a thorough survey of the shoes onboard, finally choosing some comfortable-looking Hush Puppies to sit beside. I have begun to discern the Palestinians from the Israelis on the train by their shoes; Israelis, no matter their social class, concern themselves with what brand of shoes they wear. I take this as the mark of a people who care about and nurture themselves. Palestinians don't usually care as much, and they'll wear whatever knockoffs they can get at a bargain, especially the women, who couldn't care less about comfort. Suheil was the first to draw my attention to the cheap shoes I wore, shoes we've agreed are to blame for my back pain. He only buys shoes that cost hundreds of shekels, which I used to consider bizarre. That was actually when my habit of footwear-profiling on public transportation started.

Whenever I board the train, I worry about being discovered, exposed. On the one hand, if anyone I know sees me—especially Tania or any of her Jerusalemite friends with blue IDs—they'll brand me a "normalizer," and probably lecture me on how I should boycott the light-rail system because it's designed to help expand the settlements (the line I'm on now, for example, is mainly for commuters that live in Pisgat Ze'ev). On the other hand, if the Israeli commuters realize I'm Arab, I could be subjected to all kinds of unseemly staring, and the security guard will undoubtedly ask to see my ID. The fact that I have a Jerusalem-residency permit because I'm married to a Jerusalem ID holder won't stop anyone from staring at the lack of blue on my ID card, like they're staring at the woman in the green headscarf, though she doesn't seem to pay it any mind. This is why I practice sitting in the most neutral and least terroristic way every time I use the train. Ring! The most embarrassing moments are when my phone rings, like it's doing now, especially when it's Suheil calling. Of course, it's Suheil who's calling. It's particularly annoying because he hasn't figured out that I switch to my broken English when I'm in these spaces.

"Yes, I'm in the train."

He doesn't understand what I'm saying, so I shield my mouth with my hand and whisper in Arabic, "I'm on the train, do you need something?"

"OK, I'll call you later."

I'd decided to do it today. The name of a lab on the second floor of a building across from the city hall on Yafa Street is scribbled on the corner of a piece of paper in my hand. My neighbor Amany jotted it down, explaining that this was an excellent lab and would carry out any test I wanted so long as I could pay, even if I didn't have insurance.

The Maqased Hospital has a lab equipped for this kind of test. A while back, I inquired about doing mine there, but the technician's face contorted in shock when I went into detail. I immediately became the subject of his wincing suspicions. He curtly ended the conversation, saying there would need to be a formal request from the criminal-investigation unit at the police department for such a test to be performed. I would need a bona fide crime and a police report to boot. I imagined myself at the police department reporting the suspected crime of not being my dead father's daughter.

Surely, an Israeli lab will not care, I tell myself. Still, I'm not sure how I'll explain my request when I arrive. I don't even know what language I'll use to do the explaining, especially since people often refuse to respond in English even if they speak it. The only thing I can do in Hebrew is apologize. "*Sleekha!*"

I doublecheck to make sure that the strand of Yara's hair is still in its little plastic pouch in my handbag. Yesterday as she obsessed over her furniture while yelling at Shireen for knocking the white stone-encrusted vase off the table, I snuck into her room, and pulled from her hairbrush the hair that I then stashed in the pouch. Yara entered the room abruptly, oblivious to what I'd done, only to tell me that she'd found Linda, her rival from our Tunis days. Linda had dropped out of university, she'd learned, and the sparkle in Yara's eyes expressed her jubilation at this triumph. Linda was better at school in Tunis than Yara. Even Hanoi and Zainab—who'd had to retake their general exams four times before finally passing—had eventually completed their college degrees, although one of them had failed to find a husband. Yet even after moving from Tunis to Beirut (because her mother refused to move to Jenin with her dad), Linda still hadn't managed to make much of herself.

I don't really remember my schoolmates, although I occasionally spot some of them roaming around Ramallah. When I do see them, they're usually hanging out at the bars and cafés that have suddenly popped up all over town, where they've become regulars. Most of them had failed and repeated years of high school, then gone on to fail at love and work until they finally found a little corner of life that let them eke out some satisfaction. Mr. Radwan, the science teacher, is the only one I greet when I see him, usually on his way to the National Security headquarters where he's worked since his Return. Similarly, I've heard that Mr. Mohammad Ramadan, the Arabic teacher, had a job with the police, but retired a while back. The others, well, it was as if they weren't there, as if the shoe factory in the heart of the industrial zone of Tunis that was turned into our school never existed, and everyone who'd been there had suddenly melted into the air, in spite of the Facebook page still emblazoned with the school's name.

The guard on the train hovers above me. I flash my ticket, and he scans it with the machine to confirm that it's valid, then moves on to check the next passenger. The train passes from Beit Hanina to Shu'fat, where grocers and butchers and fūl vendors and plumbers line both sides of the street. Passengers upset by seeing this many Arabs in Jerusalem gape their dismay through the windows. There's a diverse cast of characters on board the train: a young Russian woman accompanied by a young man so blond he's almost see-through; two Filipina women chatting; a Somali man holding on to a two-wheeled cart brimming with textiles; men with identical black hats and dark suits, one of them sitting across from me swaying in his seat, the other with white earphones shooting songs from his phone into his brain.

We stop in al-Sahl. A group of teens gets on. School's out, or at least that's what their heavy backpacks suggest. They sit close to one another, except for the two who don't sit down. They whisper in Arabic, and the security guard's eyes barely blink away from them while the boys are on the train. They turn their backs to him and continue their conversation about the PE teacher who punished one of them by forcing him to run laps for half an hour—at least, that's what I gather from the snippets I overhear.

The train comes to another stop at French Hill, as the recorded voice dutifully announces. A group of young women board. One is chubby and wears tight green trousers and a short fuchsia blouse; the others are dressed in matching miniskirts, polo shirts and Nike running shoes. They speak and sing and shriek in Hebrew as the schoolboys look on inquisitively. They too begin to gradually raise the volume on their own conversation. By the time the train has passed a few more stops, it has become a theater of shouts and jokes and laughs in both Arabic and Hebrew, which all the hard stares of the security guard are helpless to subdue.

A sudden lurch catches the girls off-guard, and one of them falls into the lap of one of the seated boys, who is all too grateful to cushion her landing. The roars of laughter only get louder with the girl's jolt and tumble. She takes her time getting back to her feet. This riles up the boys, who start to jealously tease the young landing pad as the girls prattle on in words I don't understand between bouts of laughter. At that moment, the guard approaches, scowling as he points to the boy, who now seems at ease. He demands that the boy take his foot off the seat, and the boy sheepishly complies without comment, rejoining his pals' merriment with a little less excitement.

I exit the train on Yafa Street, and begin my search for the lab. Amany described it as an old-looking building that was renovated, just across from the Municipality. If only she'd given me an address; everything here looks old and renovated, even the railway track that's only just been completed.

I take my chance first on one building, which sports a gallery of religious artwork on its ground floor. The staircase is narrow and dimly lit. I spot several men and a boy, all in Hasidic attire, coming down the stairs. The building is probably a school or an apartment block, so I hurry back down to try the next building. My throat feels parched suddenly, but I won't stop to drink anything because I'm fasting with the expectation that this might be a requirement for any blood test at the lab.

It's unclear where the entrance to the next building might be. It seems to have a million windows, but no doors. I walk around until I finally find a metal gate with grey, steel-latticed openings. It's locked and only opens from the inside. I ring the doorbell and a voice responds in Hebrew, so I ask in English whether someone could open the door for me. A few seconds later the door buzzes open, and I climb the stairs with my knees barely keeping me upright.

The waiting room is full, and most people there are Orthodox Jews. They're dressed in religious vestments—pregnant women, old men, women in wheelchairs. I approach the circular reception desk in the middle of the room, and attempt to speak with a blond Russian woman wearing half the world's make-up on her eyes. I've just rehearsed the English phrases to use:

"Hello, can you sbeek English?"

"*Ma?*"

"Can you sbeek English, I need to do tist."

"*Ma? Lo* English, *lo.*"

"Arabic?"

"*Lo, lo.*"

It's no use. I look around, searching for someone who can translate for me. A voice rises from behind the receptionist: a dark-skinned woman in her late forties with short, dark black hair. In broken Iraqi Arabic she says:

"What?"

"Hi, you speak Arabic?"

"A little."

"I want to do a test."

"*Kupat Holim?*"

"No, I don't have health insurance."

The woman stops and begins to translate the situation to the Russian.

"I want to do a DNA test for my sister and myself."

"Where's your sister?"

"I have one of her hairs."

"Which hair?'"

"One from her head.'"

"Where's her head?"

"On the rest of her body." I force down a smile at the absurdity of the question before she can see it.

"And why you want to do?"

"Because I want to be certain that we're sisters, 100 percent."

She stops again to translate to the receptionist, who, completely uninterested in the matter, responds with something the woman then translates:

"Where's your father?"

"Dead."

"And your mother?"

"In Lebanon."

Again, a pause for interpretation, after which she looks up and asks:

"And why do you want to do the test?"

"My blood type."

"What?'"

"AB positive."

"And your sister?"

"O positive."

"And your mother?"

"A positive."

"And your father?"

"O positive."

This feels more like an interrogation unrelated to medical matters. No one is writing anything down, and nothing is being translated.

"Do you do such tests here?"

"We'll see. Give me your ID."

Things are getting complicated now. I slowly pull out the all-important and damningly green piece of plastic-coated cardboard, while asking why it's relevant. As soon as the corner of the document is visible, the Russian snatches it, muttering something to my translator. She then picks up the phone and says more words I don't understand. My translator walks away, then comes back with a man in his late fifties. He's bald, and the top buttons of his shirt are undone, his muscles threatening to pop off the rest. She says the man will ask me some questions that she will translate, so I nod.

"Why do you want to do the test?"

"I want to make sure that I'm my sister's sister."

This is the only logical answer. My father is dead, and the man I think is my father is also dead. My mother is definitely my mother, whatever the case. The only person whose relation to me I need to confirm is my sister.

"Where's your sister?"

"At her home."

"Does she know you want to have this test done?"

"No."

"Where's your mother?"

"In Beirut."

"Why?"

"Because that's where she's from."

"And your father?"

"Dead."

"And you, where do you live?"

"In Jerusalem."

The man turns silent. He says a few more words to the nurse, then returns to his office. The woman asks me to follow her.

She enters a room, and then places a Hebrew-language questionnaire on the table in front of me, telling me I have to complete it, though we've definitely established that I know nothing of the language. I ask her to help, and she responds that she'll be back in a bit.

I remind myself why I am in this ridiculous situation. I stare blankly at the five-page questionnaire with its incomprehensible runes. Is this what will prove whether Yara is really my sister? Can a questionnaire definitively prove, or disprove, such a thing? All I can think about is that pillow soaked with our tears when my father left us at our neighbors' house in Tunis and traveled to Amman for a heart procedure. The bedsheets were scratchy with sand. Someone had gone to the beach and wiped their feet and body on this abandoned bed in the apartment of 'Ammo Zuheir and his wife on the seventh floor of our building. You don't know what it's like to sleep on a sandy bed until you've tried it. Yara and I drenched the pillow with our tears. We spoke of trivial things, then outright silly things, then fell into a fit of giddy laughter that shepherded us into sleep and a shared dream of the sea.

The woman returns with a young man in a janitor's uniform holding window-washing liquid and a rag. He'll be the one to help me fill in the questionnaire, she announces.

The fellow is from al-Khalil, and he seems pleased with his new role. He tries to offer his help with every ounce of chivalry he can muster, whether I want it or not. Still, he can't hide the shock on his face as he writes down my answers for the type of test I want and my reasons for wanting it. My regret swells with every question: family name, address, phone number, emergency contact. He clumsily attempts a comforting smile, and my soul screams in silent agony when he offers the friendly declaration, "Oh, I live very close by, in Shu'fat."

At this point I want nothing more than to leave the room. I ask him to ask the nurse why she put me in here, and to tell her that I want to leave. He pretends not to hear. If anyone is to put an end to his momentary promotion it won't be me, and his eyes say he wants the juicy details. His words confirm it when he goes on to ask about my parents and why they divorced and other questions that are far too specific to be on a clinical questionnaire.

The Iraqi woman comes back and asks that I wait a little longer. I feel suffocated, and my hungry stomach claws at my thoughts. My body screams with anxiety. I don't want the test today. I tell her that I'll come back another time, but she won't have it. I will have wasted their time for nothing, she says, and that's not acceptable. I have to carry on with the procedure.

I don't get the test done. It isn't my wits or determination that get me out of there, but my insolvency; the DNA test at this clinic costs 2,000 shekels. I leave the building in a rush, thanking my wallet for only containing the 500 shekels that I thought would be more than enough. I buy some cream-filled biscuits, finishing them in an anxious binge as I wait for the train to come and take me home.

This time I sit beside a pair of Clarks worn by a young man. It's rush hour, and we are packed in the train like sardines in a tin. I close my eyes and try to forget everything that has just happened, planning what I'll say in case Yara ever finds out what I've done. She's always said that someday something I do will make a fool of her, because I think that life is simple and I can do whatever I want. She's convinced that people are monsters and we should never let our guard down, never give anyone the chance to exploit our vulnerabilities.

The security guard arrives to check my ticket. I dig it out of my purse and hand it over. He scans it on his machine, then mutters something in the unintelligible Hebrew.

"What?" I ask in English, so he translates. My ticket is no longer valid because the hour-and-a-half window I had to make my return journey ended fifteen minutes ago. And he is going to fine me. That isn't fair, I protest, but he stolidly asks for my ID.

A young man from the opposite row of seats intervenes with some Hebrew. Eyes begin to turn toward me, but the guard repeats his demand to see my ID. I draw it out of my bag, and automatically unfold my permit as well, the pair of Clarks now dismayed and denouncing me.

I'm incensed. I have to pay a fine of 180 shekels for fifteen minutes of tardiness—me, the woman who's been unemployed for two months! The man who's intervened comes closer, and in a quiet Arabic says, "Assholes, all they want to do is siphon money from us Arabs."

The guard takes down the information on my identification documents, then hands them back with the ticket and says he's written his name and number on it in case I want to file a complaint. I look at the ticket. His name, my avenue to redress, is scribbled in Hebrew.

I get up from beside the Clarks, fearing that the tears streaming down my face will cause a scene. Everyone will think I'm crying over 180 shekels. I am, but I'm also crying for another feeling that has gripped my heart. I stand with my face flattened against the glass door of the train. I see cars and utility poles and people rushing by. I feel the cold of the glass against my forehead and the warmth of my tears trickling down one by one, salty, into my mouth.

From a distance I see Shireen rushing at me, her hand in Suheil's. She drags her little bag behind her, and with it all the dirt on the sidewalk. Our paths meet at the entrance to the building, where she leaps to my chest and asks me about the Dora doll I'd promised to buy her that morning. Needless to say, Dora was the last thing on my mind, so I promise to buy it tomorrow. She's unconvinced, so I have to add a whole plastic teatime set to the bargain.

"There go my 500 shekels," I proclaim to the ether as my eyes move toward Suheil. He's yet to ask a single question about my day.

"Don't you want to know what happened?"

"What?"

"Nothing."

"I told you to leave this nonsense be."

He asks me whether I went over to his mother's to make lunch. I hadn't, of course, and even if I had, his mother would have told me with all the certainty of tomorrow's sunrise that she'd already eaten, and the fortune I would have spent on the cab ride would have gone to waste.

I try to get Suheil to take some interest in listening to what I've been through, but he doesn't even look up from the game on his phone. When I protest, he says that I should keep talking, that he's been listening to every word.

I declare that I will get the 2,000 shekels together soon, and get the test done.

He looks up, laughing as he says, "The electricity bill is way more important than figuring out your mother and father right now."

Malika – Nina

Jerusalem, 2012

When will she stop wetting herself? I saw her do it. I know she intentionally sits on my bed, knowing full well that her clothes are wet. Why must I tolerate the flatulence bombs she shamelessly sets off in every corner of the house? If only I could make her hear me, I'd say, "Nina, aren't you ashamed, wetting yourself like that?"

You can't trick me like you trick Suheil, Nina.

You say to him—with that sad puppy-dog voice you use to soften him up—that you're old, that you forget, that you don't know what you're doing. I see you, putting your pills in that rusted old powdered-milk tin every time he gives them to you, even though he shouts himself into a migraine because you forget to take them. You clap your hands and say, "I forgot," then move on to one of your hackneyed punchlines, like: "Your aunt Malika took every pill ever made, but she still died."

Then you take whatever pills he hands you and go to the kitchen for a glass of water, only to place them, with poise and determination, in that rusty Nido tin.

You can't fool me, Nina. And I don't believe you when you sit on the sofa and declare, with that sheepish smile on your face, "I only meant to fart, but shat by mistake." Then you go to my room and sit on *my* bed, the bed you never dared go near before, none of you did, and with those clothes you've brushed against god knows what. Now you just plop your shit-stained butt on my sheets. I've even caught you waking up at night smelling filthy and then falling right back asleep without even thinking of washing yourself. How do you do it? How?

You try to convince everyone that you're forgetful, but when Suheil took you to the doctor they found no trace of Alzheimer's. He wasn't convinced and insisted you had some form of dementia. You were happy that he still cared, and that there was no one in his life to compete with you. I saw you going into my room. I saw you looking at the framed portrait of me above the heater, and I saw you flick your middle finger at it.

I no longer sleep, so I watch you sleep. In the morning you wake up frightened. You look up at the image of the Virgin and pray that she forgives your sins. You go to the sink, splash some water on your face, then polish your dentures by rubbing them with your palm before putting them in your mouth without even a glance at the mirror.

You sit on the sofa to go back to sleep, until Um Sami knocks on the door with the tip of her wooden stick to inquire whether you're dead yet. When she sees your outline through the glass door she wryly exclaims, "You're still with us, I see!"

And you respond, "Someone needs to stick around to sit on your chest."

She retorts by praying that you die soon so she can get her house back and rent it out for a hundred times what you pay. You tell her—as you tell her every day—that the only way you'll leave is flat on your back. She then curses the day she accepted your husband as a tenant 40 years ago, and you pretend not to have heard her when you declare that you entered the house as a bride and will leave it only as a corpse.

Then you go to the courtyard together to have the coffee that the barber's wife makes for you, each of you telling stories that have nothing to do with the house or the rent. I hear these stories repeated time and again without the right to interrupt and correct you, even when you start to rework them, shoving one story up the ass of another, muddling them all together however you like.

You tell four stories, the same four you'll repeat all day.

Before I metamorphosed into what I am now, you had more stories, and they were more fun to hear, stories of mothers-in-law and daughters-in-law. I particularly liked the story with the punchline, "She might have looked like my daughter, but she had my daughter-in-law's bum." You told stories of mothers-in-law who made the lives of their daughters-in-law a living hell, affirming your status as the ideal mother-in-law because you didn't ask any of your three sons' wives to produce the bloodied bedsheet to prove their premarital virginity. Then there was that other story about the husband who lived with his wife and her sister: the two women took turns bearing children, registering all the newborns as children of the married sister. Then you'd announce, while glaring at me from the corner of your angry eye, that they all still lived in the same house until this day.

You'd often tell the story of the palm reader, a tale you considered magical and mysterious, and which led you to stress that your marriage to a Muslim was fated, somehow beyond your control. After all, you'd proclaim, it had been predicted fifteen years before you met the man you would marry. The palmist had said you'd marry a "stranger" from whom you'd beget an odd number of children: one or three or five. You'd then triumphantly unveil that all this came true. You married a Muslim and bore him three sons as prophesied.

So many stories. In those other days I would have interrupted to correct you, especially when you forgot the main hook, the detail that made the story worth hearing, or if you jumbled two stories into one. My memory was solid as metal and my interventions were always on point. "That's not how it went, you idiot." I'd then retell it with everything in its place, no details missing, no details added. You'd protest, of course, "How should I know, does my brain look like a ledger book to you?"

Then we might get into a fight, or not, depending on what else had happened that day. Sometimes in the middle of a story I might even get riled up, like I am right now as I watch you regale these weary women, each waiting her turn to do some complaining, reminiscing, and nagging of her own. At those times I'd tell a completely different story, like the story of the sheep's head that a Jordanian notable served on top of the massive platter of mansaf when his wife gave birth to a boy at the Hospice Hospital. Or the story of Hilmy Basem Ra'ed, a name spelled out to Abu Suheil while I curiously looked on as he recorded it in the birth registry, not knowing what the name meant. I took it to be Raqed, like the word for sleeping, but Abu Suheil corrected me. He said it was like the word for leader, like Jamal Abdel Nasser, the ra'ed of the Arab nation. He got so excited about the name that he gave it to our second son.

When I told my stories, you didn't dare breathe a word. You'd sit and stare at the television, or maybe get up and wander aimlessly around the house.

Now you doggedly tell these stories: the first, about how the priest declared that you'd need a document proving your divorce from Abu Suheil before he could re-baptize you. Only then could you become a Christian again and be buried beside me in the Greek Orthodox cemetery. You then look at

Suheil and say some choice words. "Don't go burying me with the Muslims, I swear I'll jump out of my grave. And don't go writing your father's name on my tombstone. Katrina Lambi Khorgioli, daughter of Lambi Khorgioli, that's what you'll write." Suheil nods his head, still glued to the game on his phone. If he's in the mood, he'll tease you, "Then you'd be an apostate, and the Muslims would kill you. In any case, you're the most Muslim person I know because you took yourself to the court and declared your fealty to Islam. Everyone else became Muslim because they were born into it."

Agitated, you shout, "Listen here, you Muslim punk, I'm a Christian through and through. Curse the day your father tricked me into marrying him. You really are a Muslim seed, a dirty rotten seed."

Suheil laughs. You don't.

Your second story generally revolves around your pension payments, which come in at the beginning of each month and are promptly lost somewhere between you picking up the cash from Bank Leumi on Salah al-Din Street and getting back home. No one knows where the money goes, but we're certain it's somewhere in the house because it's most likely that you hide it, then forget the hiding place. That, or you know where it is and won't say. The important point is that you make everyone waste their day scouring the house for the money. The next day you invariably head to the bank, where they confirm that you did indeed pick up the payment, then you shuttle back home to plough through the 50 or so handbags, each stored in its own white plastic bag wrapped in another black plastic bag, all in the hope that the money might turn up.

But I know where you bury your 1,000-shekel treasure. It's in the red purse, the one you keep in a white plastic bag that you wrap in a black plastic bag before stowing it behind the half-empty whiskey bottle in my closet.

You come back an hour later to move it somewhere else, stashing it under your bed. Then you call Suheil to announce that you want to go pick up your pension. He tells you that you just went to the bank and already made the withdrawal. You insist that you haven't, that you can't find the money.

When this first started happening, Suheil would turn the house upside-down looking for the money. Then he suspected that someone was stealing it. Then he finally realized that his mother was probably hiding it somewhere and forgetting, despite her insistence that she never has and never would hide money, and that she never goes into my room or messes around in my closet, even now that I'm dead.

Your third story is the one about our mother. This story, as you tell it to Jumana every time she visits, is that our mother—who you always refer to as "mama, may God's anger hail down upon her"—married a Coptic Egyptian after divorcing our father, a man fifteen years her elder.

"My father was as jealous as my mother was beautiful. He would beat her and swear at her using the nastiest words. He had a foul mouth, God rest his soul," you would say.

You'd then drift onto another topic. "Malika is the reason I married Abu Suheil. If she hadn't bought that plot of land that day, if she hadn't taken our sister Marika and I along, I wouldn't have met him, and none of it would have happened."

Your face reddens when you describe the young bachelor who would become Abu Suheil. "He was a land broker in those days. I'd seen an ad he'd placed at the cinema, and Marika and I called him hoping to buy some land with money we'd been saving from our salaries. He would say sweet words to me, and take me to the cinema. One day he took me to his office in Ramallah. He was tall like Rushdy Abaza. He took me by the waist and kissed me on the lips, and from that day on I was ensnared. We ran away together, I converted to Islam, and we got married."

You then rue that day. "Dirty Muslims! Curse the day I met him. Accusing me of stealing the servant's jewelry."

Your mind drifts again. "My father was angry because I married a Muslim, and the Greeks were scandalized. He almost disowned me in the church, the way Abu Hanna did with his daughter, but Malika convinced him not to."

You then curse Abu Suheil, who married his secretary in Amman and left you to live all alone in this big house. You will go to the court in the Old City with Marika, you announce. You will get your divorce and humiliate him in the newspapers with an ad that reads: "Faisal Khalil Shuqair, son of Abu Faisal, left his wife for the maid, his wife's sister." You force out an uneasy laugh, asking Suheil if that's something you can actually do. Suheil doesn't usually respond because he doesn't listen to half of what you say. When he does, it's to say "no, mom, it's not something you can do." You lose yourself, silent in your thoughts for a while, then perk up. "I'm going to do it tomorrow anyway."

I sit across from you, no clue what you're thinking.

"Nina, say something!"

But you don't respond. Why don't you ask Suheil what his father is up to anymore? Why don't you berate him for the fact that he doesn't call? Why don't you curse his father and mother like you usually would? Why don't you do anything? I sit across from you, despite your soul-crushing smell.

"Maggots will start coming out your butthole, Nina."

I can hear the response in your thoughts. "Your obsession with being 'clean' is what shut you up."

Only the clock's ticktock breaks the silence of your restless naps on the sofa. The TV screen is now just a blank mirror, no longer a conveyor of wholesome delights.

"Turn on the damned television, Nina! Let's have a bit of fun."

You respond with a snore, slouching into the sofa with your legs propped up on the coffee table. Your head hangs to the side, the corner of your mouth crusted with dried drool.

"Open the damned window, Nina! Your filth has gorged itself on the house."

You turn your gaze toward the wall, toward the spot where a picture of a five-year-old Suheil in his Greek caftan and fez hangs.

"Prime the lamp to summon the light, Nina!"

You adjust your position, crossing one leg over the other. You sink your cheek into your palm and doze back into oblivion.

"Turn on the light, Nina! You know I hate the dark."

You leave me, dragging yourself into the bedroom.

"It's only seven o'clock, Nina."

You look to the Virgin above your bed.

"Good night, our Mother."

"The phone is ringing, Nina, answer it!"

You run to the phone, nimble as a four-year-old girl.

"Yes, habibi, I ate."

"No, you didn't!"

"Yes, I took my medicine."

"You did nothing of the sort."

"Yes, dear, the red pill."

"You liar, don't lie to the boy. Go in and take your damned medicine."

"I'm on the sofa, sweetie, where else would I be?"

"You were getting into bed, you wretched crone. Tell him! Give me that phone. Just you wait until I get my hands on you."

You hang up, recite the line you mutter to yourself after each of his calls: "That boy might as well put on a damned dog-collar and hand his wife the leash."

122

Then you worm into bed, and the symphony of snores promptly begins.

"Do you remember when we used to ditch school and head to the cemetery to smoke with Marika?"

"The principal found us, she told mother."

"You got it good that day."

"You played innocent, and I got the whipping."

"Because I'm the youngest."

"When are you going to tell him?"

"Nina, wake up, it's already morning."

Um Mohammad enters the flat, raising a storm in the dormant house. She moves around like a rocket. There are, after all, five other geriatric women whose posteriors need to be relieved of their soiled diapers. She yanks off her veil with one swift motion, then produces a loaf of ka'ek from a steam-filled black plastic bag. The heady aroma of toasted sesame confirms that it's from the bakery in Musrara. She rips the loaf in half. You insist that you've already had breakfast but she knows your games as well as anyone else. She moves like a machine, deaf to your incessant objections, and pushes the warm piece of bread into your palm. She darts into the bathroom and whisks open the shower curtain, unsettling a shower of mildewed dry paint that snows down from the ceiling onto her hair. She capers into the bedroom and sets out a clean diaper and some wool trousers on the bed, does a pirouette behind your bedroom door to grab that tattered imported towel (the one you insist on using instead of any one of the perfectly fine towels folded on the shelf above the steel ring in the bathroom) and places the towel neatly beside the bathtub. In a flash, she's back at your side. She yanks the unpecked piece of ka'ek from your hand, and muffles your protests by shoving a piece into your mouth before launching into the familiar invective about how you need to take the shower you so adamantly refuse. Gulping down the bread, you insist that you really do wash yourself every day.

"Anyway I'm baptized, and baptized people don't get stinky like Muslims."

Um Mohammad forces out a throaty laugh as she strips off your trousers, then deftly undoes your diaper with an expert flick of her hand. She pulls off your red turtleneck, leaving your grey hair tufting like a scraggy broom. The mighty grip of her hand drags you toward the tub as you pull at your hair and slap your own face with your free hand in protest, howling about how you bathed last night and reminding her of perpetual purity imparted by the baptismal font. Your protests are futile; she has learned that assisting the elderly is neither the time nor the place for discussion and debate. What they say may often be true, but it's rarely important. No one cares what they say. The sons keep conversation within the bounds of very particular and highly controlled topics—mainly, taking medicine on time and eating regular meals. The daughters are mostly concerned with the house being clean and the hair being neat. Um Mohammad evaluates the situation of each of her clients, then deals with them on the basis of her assessment. The showerhead is activated, and Nina summarily placed beneath it.

"Wait for the water to get warm first!" I try to scream at Um Mohammad, but she has no time for such subtleties. Nina doesn't feel the cold. Instead, she stands in surrender, vanquished after all, and limp like everything else about her. Um Mohammad squeezes a blob of shampoo onto Nina's head and scrubs it into her scalp, repeating as one would to a child, "There you go, lovely girl, now you'll be beautiful."

She dries her with rapid movements of the towel that crisscross Nina's body, then leads her, naked, to the bedroom.

"Legs, please."

Nina spreads them and raises her hips, and Um Mohammad wraps the diaper. She then dresses her in the trousers that she'd already laid out on the bed, and asks Nina to select a light nightshirt since the heat has set in. Nina is adamant that she has no such nightshirt and that she feels cold. Um Mohammad obliges, continuing the ritual with an undershirt and a blue turtleneck. She plugs the blow dryer into the outlet, and positions Nina between her legs to dry her hair as if in a race with the wind. A minute later, she hands Nina her morning pill, then glides towards the door, dexterously whipping her shawl back onto her head, covering her hair before reaching the door. Her next client is the venerable hajjeh Um Fathy, who lives at the very end of Nabi Ya'qoub Street, and Um Mohammad is right on schedule.

You sink into position on the sofa. Unprompted, you get up and scuttle to the door. A look through the peephole confirms that Um Sami is not coming to find out if you're dead yet. You resume your vigil on the sofa.

"Where is that curmudgeon? Gone without a word or a trace."

After that you go quiet again, Nina, and silence is my only companion once again.

Suheil opens the door, walking in with Jumana and Shireen in tow.

"Kaliméra, Mama."

"Kaliméra, habibi."

"Christ is risen."

"He is truly risen. But why dear? What's today?"

"It's Eid, ma, we talked about this, and you said you'd get ready so we can go out."

"I don't know."

"Just get up and get ready so we can have lunch together."

"No, habibi, I can't go out today."

"Why, what else do you have in your dayplanner?"

"What about your aunt?"

"My aunt's been dead for four years, ma."

I get in the car beside Suheil, between you and him. I place my head on his shoulder. He's busy driving, and biting his nails.

"When are you going to stop that gross habit?"

Jumana clutches her belly with one hand, and places the other in front of her mouth as if she's about to vomit.

"You're pregnant, girl! You're in the eighth week."

Nina opens her handbag every five minutes looking through her four wallets for the house key. She finds it, returns it to the bag she then zips closed, only to start the hunt again a short while later.

The car heads towards Ra'uf wa Atena, the famous seaside restaurant in Yafa. Shireen and Jumana have fallen asleep in the back, and Nina is back to fumbling with her handbag, looking for her key. Suheil lets out a burst of anger at the driver in front of him who's blocking the lane and not allowing us to get past.

Tel Aviv – 34km announces the white text on the green road sign in Arabic and Hebrew.

Shireen wakes up crying, "I want go pee pee." Jumana sits up and asks Suheil to pull over, but Suheil, obsessed as he is with traffic laws, refuses to stop anywhere but the next exit.

"Suheil, she's about to wet herself again," pleads Jumana, whose hormones can't bear an argument right now.

Suheil parks under the big road sign pointing to the Modi'in settlement. Shireen gets out of the car, triumphant. She bends her knees to distance her hips from her feet like an Olympic champion in the sport of roadside urination. Down pours a steamy stream that parts the soil, not stopping until it forms a small pool at the foot of the sign.

NOTES

Um 'Aziz

8: In many parts of the Arab world Abu (father, father of) and Um (mother, mother of) are used to form nicknames, as well as a person's kinya, a way of referring to the person by the name of their eldest son, although there are plenty of exceptional cases in which people take on the name of their eldest daughter in their kinya (e.g., George Habash of the Popular Front for the Liberation of Palestine was known as Aby Maysa). So, a couple with the eldest son Aziz would be called Abu 'Aziz (father of 'Aziz) and Um 'Aziz (mother of 'Aziz). Addressing someone using their kinya is a way of signaling familiarity without necessarily being too formal or intimate. It is not uncommon for boys and childless men to have a kinya that refers to the name they're expected to give their son, as is the case with Abu al-Saeed later in this story. It is also important to note that *noms de guerre* in the Palestine Liberation Organization (PLO) were in the form of kinyas, the most notable being Yasser Arafat: Abu Ammar.

not allowed to enter Jerusalem

10: As of about 2003, Israel's pass-law system has forbidden Palestinians with West Bank or Gaza IDs from entering Jerusalem without a permit from the Israeli military. Israeli authorities classify Palestinians who can demonstrate that their "center of life" is the city of Jerusalem as "permanent residents" of the state of Israel, and they carry special blue-colored "Jerusalem" IDs. Jerusalem-ID Palestinians are regularly stripped of these IDs and their residency rights. That no one can visit the father indicates that all who would visit him carry West Bank IDs (or are refugees not allowed into the country at all), and those on West Bank IDs can only enter Jerusalem with special permits from the military.

military commander for el-Munazzameh

14: *El-Munazzameh* (literally, "the Organization") is the common shorthand for Munazzamat al-Tahrir al-Filistiniya, the Palestine Liberation Organization (PLO).

an aspiring fida'i

15: Plural: *fida'iyyin*. A prosaic way of saying "those who sacrifice." This became the main way to refer to Palestinian fighters in the militant factions of the PLO, and has been used as a descriptor for militants in other struggles across the Arab world. Often translated as "commandos" or "guerrillas," and often rendered in English as "Fedayeen."

Ra'fat al-Hajjan

15: The wildly popular late 1980s Egyptian TV series based on the book of the same name by Saleh Mursi. Both book and series offer a semi-fictionalized account of the adventures of Ref'at al-Jammal, Egypt's most famous secret agent spying on Israel. Al-Jammal used the alias Jack Beton as he collected crucial information for Egyptian intelligence over a period of almost two decades.

eight piastres

16: The main unit of Jordanian currency is the dinar, made up of 100 piastres (*qurush*, singular: *qirsh*).

Abu al-Hol

16: The *nom de guerre* of Hayil Abdelhamid, one of the founding members of Fateh, and later its security chief. Fateh was the dominant faction of the PLO, headed by Yasser Arafat from its founding in 1959 until his death in 2004, and is often rendered "Fatah" in English. Israeli commandos assassinated Abdelhamid in Tunis in 1991. Abu al-Hol is also the Arabic name of the Sphinx in Giza, Egypt.

kufiyyeh

18: Patterned headscarf, also known as a *hatta*, that came to be associated with the Palestinian struggle since the uprising against British rule and Zionist colonization in the second half of the 1930s.

tahina

19: Sesame paste. Also transliterated *tahini* following the Lebanese and northern Palestinian pronunciation.

shatta

19: A saucy paste of slightly fermented chilis in a blend of olive oil, herbs, and spices.

fūl

20: Pronounced *fool*, the name for fava beans, usually eaten mashed with some combination of fresh tomato, garlic, cumin, onions, and often cilantro or parsley (or on their own with some salt and olive oil). The *fawwal*, or *fūl* vendor, is where you'd go to get inexpensive variants of mashed *fūl*, hummus, and falafel in platter or sandwich form.

the September War

20: Also known as the "Jordanian Civil War" or "Black September," this was the 1970–1971 showdown between Jordanian monarchists and a coalition of pan-Arabists and anti-imperialists centered around the militant factions of the PLO.

mukhabarat

22: State intelligence agencies.

mulukhiya

27: Mulukhiya is the dark green leaves of jute mallow (*corchorus olitorius*). It is prepared and eaten in different ways from the Caribbean and tropical and northern Africa to India and Southeast Asia. In Jordan it has come to be associated with Palestinians in particular, owing to its prominence in Palestinian cuisine, whether finely minced, coarsely chopped, or left whole. The "correct" way of preparing the dish is hotly contested. It has recently gained popularity as a "superfood" in Japan as *moroheiya*.

Eid

28: Literally: festive occasion. This is the word used for all religious holidays, including Eid al-Fitr (festival of breaking the fast, bringing the month of Ramadan to an end), also known as the small Eid because it is three days long; Eid al-Adha (festival of the sacrifice), also known as the long Eid because it lasts four days; Eid al-Milad (festival of the birth) is Christmas, and Eid al-Fiseh (Easter, "fiseh" taken from the Greek word for Easter, "Pascha," itself derived from the Hebrew Pesach for Passover).

al-Raouché

29: The westernmost tip of Beirut's coastal strip, with cliffside cafés overlooking the iconic Pigeon Rock.

tamriyyeh

37: A Palestinian dessert from the Nablus and Tulkarem area in central Palestine, in which sweetened semolina flavored with rose or orange blossom water is wrapped in sweetened dough and deep fried.

onion market

37: The different quarters in the old walled cities of the eastern Mediterranean are often named after a particular kind of commerce (e.g. the roasters' market, the onion market, and so on). They are as residential as they are commercial, and in many cases are no longer the main marketplace for the types of goods that gave them their names.

Ein al-Hilweh camp

37: The largest Palestinian refugee camp in Lebanon, on the outskirts of Saida (Sidon). A major center of Palestinian resistance history.

fourteen cards to each of the four players

38: "Hand" is a two-deck variant of gin rummy and very popular with the generation that grew up in the 1970s and '80s.

bamia
39: Okra, usually prepared in a herb-infused tomato sauce.

original Gazan
39: Since the 1948 expulsions, two-thirds of Gaza's population has been made up of Palestinian refugees from the surrounding areas. Among Palestinians, Gazan cuisine is notorious for its incorporation of hot chilis, though there is far more to Gaza's cuisine than fiery heat.

tabbuleh
39: A fresh cold salad of finely chopped parsley and raw onion, tomato and soaked bulgur with a dressing of olive oil and squeezed lemon popular across greater Syria. As with tahina/tahini, it often appears on European language menus as tabouli.

Lebanese-style kubbeh
39: *Kubbeh* usually refers to mincemeat and onions (often with pine nuts) cooked and enveloped into an elliptical shape with a mixture of finely minced meat and bulgur that's fried until crisp and crunchy on the outside. *Kubbeh nayyeh* (literally raw, or tartare) is the mincemeat, bulgur, and onion mixture served raw, a delicacy.

baba ghannouj
40: Eggplants grilled until soft and smoky, puréed with tahina, lemon and garlic (at least).

fattoush
40: A garden salad with croutons made of pita bread, fried or drizzled with olive oil and baked to a crisp. Sumac and/or pomegranate molasses are commonly held to be essential ingredients of the salad.

labaneh
45: Strained yogurt, with a consistency similar to thick cream cheese.

al-Khityar

46: Literally: the old man, one of the many nicknames for Yasser Arafat. Arafat jokes form an entire subgenre of joke, within which jokes about the PLO chairman's thick lips, and his penchant for kissing people with them, hold pride of place.

Nahr al-Bared

47: Literally: cold river, Nahr al-Bared camp is the northernmost Palestinian refugee camp in Lebanon, just outside Tripoli, and takes its name from the small river beside which it was built. In 2007, the Lebanese military leveled most of the camp in a battle against a few dozen fighters calling themselves "Fateh al-Islam."

Ragheb Alama, Rabih el-Khawli, and Sherihan in those Ramadan riddle shows

57: Some of the leading musical celebrities of the 1980s. Both Palestinian-Lebanese singer Rabih el-Khawli and Lebanese singer Ragheb Alama were graduates of the televised singing contests on the Lebanese show "Studio al-Fann" (The Arts' Studio). Sherihan was a film, television, and theater actress and dancer. Her 1984 *Fawazeer al-Amthal* (The Proverb Riddles) were among the pioneering works of the *fawazeer* Ramadan genre: after the fast breaking each night of the holy month, families across the Arab world gathered in front of the television to watch these highly ornate and choreographed variety shows in which each episode featured a particular riddle or puzzle. The queen of the genre was Lebanese-Armenian entertainer Nelly Artin Kalfayan (famous Nelly), who starred in seven different *fawazeer* shows between 1980 and 2001.

darija

58: *Darija* is the term used in Morocco, Mauritania, Tunisia, and Algeria to refer to the array of vernacular Arabic dialects of northwest Africa. It incorporates elements and vocabulary from Imazighen languages and dialects as well as French.

'Ammo Nur

59: The colloquial for "uncle." This is how young people are expected to address older men. Referring to someone as 'Ammo in their absence can also signify a degree of familiarity with an older man.

if you abandon the cause, it will abandon you
59: *al-Qadiyyah* ("the cause," or "the case" as in a legal setting), the Palestinian *Qadiyyah* (*al-Qadiyyah al-Filistiniyah*) is how Arabs commonly refer to the Palestinian struggle or the Palestine Question.

a real-life Sally
60: One of many Arabic-dubbed Japanese anime series broadcast via Arab state TV channels. *Sally* was the Arabic dub of Fumio Kurokawa's 1985 *Shoukoujo Sara*, an adaptation of Frances Hodgson Burnett's *A Little Princess*.

fattet-hummus
66: A genre of dishes in which often-stale bread is softened in broth, sauce, or yogurt. One of its most common variants is hummus fatteh, where the moisture of the chickpeas (hummus) softens the bread.

awarmah
66: From the Turkish *kavurma*, in which fatty cuts of lamb (especially from the tail) are dry fried to render the fat in which the meat cooks.

al-Fakhani
70: Al-Fakhani was the Beirut neighborhood where the PLO had its headquarters.

three-month waiting period
73: Within the Islamic legal framework, *al-'iddah* (the period of waiting) is the time a woman has to wait after a divorce (or the death of her spouse) before she can legally marry again; a period of about three months.

thoom
77: A garlic dip involving large amount of garlic blended with oil and lemon; particularly beloved in combination as a dip for grilled chicken and anything battered and deep-fried. Also called *muthawwameh* or *mtawwameh*.

Bashir Gemayel

84: Commander of the Lebanese fascist Phalange Party and son of the party founder Pierre Gemayel. In 1977 he founded the Lebanese Forces (*el-Uwwet el-Libneniyeh*), which started as the Israel-backed coalition of the different Christian supremacist groups in the country and became the main military rival of the PLO forces in Lebanon. After the Israeli invasion and occupation, and backed by the US and Israel, he was elected to the Presidency of Lebanon in late August 1982, and assassinated three weeks later by Habib Shartouni, a member of the Syrian Social Nationalist Party. The perpetrators of the Sabra and Shatila massacres framed those massacres as retaliation for Gemayel's assassination.

the Agency

86: *al-Wakalah* (the Agency) is how people often refer to UNRWA, the United Nations Relief and Works Agency for Palestine Refugees in the Near East, which has been the main international body responsible for aid and assistance to Palestinian refugees since its creation in 1949.

basterma

90: Highly seasoned cured beef with a very dark red color served in thin slices. The word "pastrami" and the slices of meat it signifies are variants.

like Darwish says

100: The reference is to Mahmoud Darwish's 1983 poem "In Praise of the Lofty Shadow."

mansaf

118: Usually served on massive platters for large numbers of guests, *mansaf* is a heaping bed of rice on top of flatbread, topped with chunks of lamb and ladled with a yogurt sauce prepared with ghee and the lamb broth used to rehydrate blocks of rock-hard sundried yogurt (*jameed*). It's often served with a garnish of roasted almonds and pine nuts, and minced parsley. The dish is typical of Bedouin herding communities and their agriculturalist neighbors in southern Palestine, and is considered the national dish in Jordan.

Raqed/Ra'ed

118: The letter *qaf* (ق) is pronounced in many different ways across the different dialects of the Arabic language. Its pronunciation as a glottal stop (like the *hamza*) is particularly common in urban dialects of the Arab Eastern Mediterranean, including Jerusalem.

Rushdy Abaza

120: Egyptian actor and heartthrob who starred in dozens of films throughout the 1950s, '60s and '70s.

I first heard of this book when Dalia Taha was visiting Brooklyn and recommended it to my housemate at the time, Ali Issa. She later gifted Ali the copy I would borrow and read for the first time. A few pages into the text, I realized that I had begun not only reading the Arabic, but also imagining what it would feel like in English. A few pages more, and an English translation felt urgent, not just what it would feel like but what it would mean. Dalia agreed, and introduced me to her friend, the author. Maya immediately gave the translation project her blessing. That was in 2015, and Maya's unflinching enthusiasm and support for this translation project, and the way you can feel her somehow smile through the phone, have been its bedrock since. We have yet to meet in person.

The plot is splattered around the ways blood and national identity serve as determinants of human relations, determinants that bureaucracies and militaries construct and exploit to administer what is at the core of human bonds, to police the very borders of life. By the end of the story, we have witnessed the failure of these determinants, which we can't help but see as flat, superficial, coercively imposed. Like Jumana, we are left with nothing but stories, secrets, songs, rumors, and lies that emerge as somehow far more concrete, and immensely more real, than the categories on ID cards and population registry spreadsheets, even when those stories are conflicting, confusing, or half-forgotten.

What first struck me about this book, and urged me to translate it into English, was what the text was not, what it is not. Unlike a great deal of writing that emerges from communities bonded by dehumanizing, racializing trauma, it is not a text that aims to argue for the humanity of its characters, or outline the brutality of colonialism and the inalienable rights of the colonized, or attempt to illustrate the cruelty of gender or any other kind of oppression. It wasn't written to illustrate victimhood. It does not plead. It just assumes the grotesque facets of the workings of power, and conducts its conversation with whoever recognizes themselves as already in the fight.

What do we center when we want to speak to *us*? When we're not trying to tell others about what we fight against and what we fight for when we fight for freedom? What questions do we want to ask together? Maya centers us around the body of the girl and woman rather than the battlefield of History and the dialectic of colonizer and colonized (though never pretending she has the privilege to ignore the colonial context in which that body is forced to exist). As she leads us in pursuit of the noisome workings of power behind closed doors, we're left with a set of questions that don't sit so comfortably on the national agenda: what is an anticolonial movement when it is at the expense of its people's autonomy, and particularly women's autonomy over their own bodies? Why do we lionize the figure of the revolutionary militant when that militant is, however understandably, transformed into a monster when it comes to those they supposedly love and cherish? Why aren't questions about motherhood and fatherhood, sisterhood and kinship, love and friendship at the core of conversations about liberty and freedom? If they were, how would that change our notion of emancipation… should it change our conception of resistance?

These were questions I was asking myself, perhaps a bit incoherently at the time I first read this book, and more coherently since, and because of. But if these are our questions for us, and if we take "us" to mean "Palestinian," why translate this to English at all? As a majority exile society, one whose colonizer's strategic objectives revolve primarily around ensuring that as few of us remain anywhere near the land that unites us as possible, to be Palestinian is not necessarily to read Arabic. Now entering a fifth generation since the Nakba, many of us are in the non-Arabic-immersed *shatat*, the Dispersion, left to figure out for ourselves what it means to be us. That inside–outside dynamic across our society globally is one of the least discussed aspects of us-ness, between those that experience the effects of Zionism as the wildly variable experience of exile and statelessness, to those that experience it as the fascism of a settler majority planting its flags wherever the eye can turn, to those that experience it as direct military and settler occupation, ghettoization, and mass incarceration, to those that experience it as soul-crushing siege and now genocide. Maya's story moves us across some of these positionalities, and my hope is that in English (and the other languages it will hopefully appear in) this book can reach not only the other diasporics, but also all the others to whom conversations about the darker side of a multigenerational collective struggle feel nothing less than crucial. Collective struggles have much to learn from one another, and the differences often have far more to teach than the similarities.

Since my first conversation with Maya, several people have stepped in with different kinds of help. The initial translation was quite terrible given how much of my academic phrasing and vocabulary kept creeping in, especially weird when the phrases were the thoughts of an eight-year-old Jumana and a teenage Yara. I am grateful to Sara Marzagora for graciously encouraging that earliest draft. The second round of drafts were kindly read by Kelly Falconer, whose feedback made me feel like it was ready to be seen by publishers. I submitted the draft to the PEN/Heim Translation Award in 2017 and received their nomination for the New York State Council of the Arts Award. How hurtful it was to see PEN's silence, and silencing, in the face of genocide as I worked to finalize the manuscript for publication.

Fady Joudah supported this project from its very early days, stepping in with some much needed, and forever appreciated, advice on publishers to approach and how to approach them. Getting minimal initial response (and a fair bit of encouraging *that's the world of publishing for you*s), the project took a backseat until the pandemic and lockdown when Diana Salman offered to read the Arabic and English side by side. Her feedback pulled me back to Jumana, Yara, Amahl, Shireen, and Abu al-Saeed, and our conversations about some of the divergences between the original and the translation helped me become more intentional about *when*s and *why*s of straying from a literal translation. Diana was also the stalwart defender of the endnotes. A well-timed award from the Laura Bassi Scholarship in the form of edits on the penultimate (Jumana) chapter, and a few friends stepping in to read through and share thoughts on all or part of the manuscript—I can't thank Minxi Chua, Dina Omar, Frida Wahbeh and Francisca Fuentes enough for their help getting to a manuscript I felt good sending out.

A special thanks to those who offered help in the final stretch: Assel Ahmad for a fun conversation about the endnotes, and what really makes fattoush *fattoush*; Malak Mattar for sharing her work *The Gathering* for the cover; Eman Abdelhadi for the final read-through and finding those typos that always seem to hide in plain sight; and to everyone at the CSU Poetry Center, who made it look easy while weathering the sudden disappearance of their (former) distribution company. Now that the book is finally in print, I can, hopefully, get Mai Taha's thoughts on it, *bas shukran istibāqan*.

Two readers in particular helped this translation get past the finish line. Amal Rammah jumped right into the story, in Maya's Arabic and my English. Our conversations about how she related to the book's stories helped keep it all alive when it could have just become words on a page. Hilary Plum showed an excitement and understanding of *No One Knows Their Blood Type* that immediately made me feel that she was the editor this book needed. Her generosity, thoughtfulness, mastery of her own craft, political integrity, and the patience and grace needed these last months redefined for me what an editor can and should be, and this text is all the better for it... shukran Hilary.

May this book contribute in some way to a better understanding of our societies and our struggles, and may that understanding be a weapon wielded against those who work to exterminate us, our memory, and our future, and may the Shireens of this world witness the freedom and justice that their mothers did not have.

HJ
June 2024

Born in 1980 in Lebanon, **Maya Abu Al-Hayyat** is an Arabic-language Palestinian novelist, poet, and children's book author. She edited *The Book of Ramallah*, an anthology of short stories published by Comma Press in 2021. Her children's book *A Blue Pond of Questions* was translated into English and published by Penny Candy Books. An English translation of her poetry appeared from Milkweed Editions under the title *You Can Be the Last Leaf*, translated by Fady Joudah and named a finalist for the National Book Critics Circle Award.

Born about a year after Maya, **Hazem Jamjoum** is a cultural historian who spends his daytimes as an audio curator and preservation archivist in London. He is an editor with the recently established publishing house Maqam Editions. His translation of Ghassan Kanafani's *The Revolution of 1936–1939 in Palestine* was published by 1804 Press in 2023. *No One Knows Their Blood Type* is his first literary translation.

RECENT CLEVELAND STATE UNIVERSITY POETRY CENTER PUBLICATIONS

edited by Caryl Pagel & Hilary Plum

POETRY

Mechanical Bull by Rennie Ament

World'd Too Much: The Selected Poetry of Russell Atkins
ed. Kevin Prufer and Robert E. McDonough

Advantages of Being Evergreen by Oliver Baez Bendorf

The Devil's Workshop by Xavier Cavazos

Ordinary Entanglement by Melissa Dickey

Dream Boat by Shelley Feller

My Fault by Leora Fridman

Orient by Nicholas Gulig

Twice There Was A Country by Alen Hamza

Age of Glass by Anna Maria Hong

outside voices, please by Valerie Hsiung

In One Form to Find Another by Jane Lewty

50 Water Dreams by Siwar Masannat

Mule: 10th Anniversary Edition by Shane McCrae

daughterrarium by Sheila McMullin

The Bees Make Money in the Lion by Lo Kwa Mei-en

Residuum by Martin Rock

Festival by Broc Rossell

Sun Cycle by Anne Lesley Selcer

Arena by Lauren Shapiro

Bottle the Bottles the Bottles the Bottles by Lee Upton

Innocence by Michael Joseph Walsh

No Doubt I Will Return A Different Man by Tobias Wray

ESSAYS

I Liked You Better Before I Knew You So Well
by James Allen Hall

A Bestiary by Lily Hoang

Codependence by Amy Long

Telephone: Essays in Two Voices
by Brenda Miller and Julie Marie Wade

The Leftovers by Shaelyn Smith

TRANSLATIONS

Almost Obscene by Raúl Gómez Jattin,
translated by Katherine M. Hedeen and Olivia Lott

Scorpionic Sun by Mohammed Khaïr-Eddine,
translated by Conor Bracken

I Burned at the Feast: Selected Poems of Arseny Tarkovsky,
translated by Philip Metres and Dimitri Psurtsev

for a complete list of titles visit CSUPoetryCenter.com